Praise for

# Billy Coffey

"SNOW DAY is the kind of book you savor, then read again. Simple, yet profound. Spare, but beautiful. Coffey chronicles a day in the life of an ordinary man who grows in extraordinary ways through simple interaction with the people and world around him. I loved this book."

—Mary DeMuth, author of the Defiance
Texas trilogy and *Thin Places*

"Billy Coffey has a way of writing that draws you into his story, which then allows you to find yourself in it. In this book he'll encourage you to pay attention, to laugh, and to wonder."

—Vince Antonucci, author of *I Became a Christian
and All I Got Was this Lousy T-Shirt*

"Set against a Blue Ridge Mountain backdrop, peopled with a colorful cast, and seasoned with small-town Southern charm, Billy Coffey's SNOW DAY will make readers want to live aware—to discover the divine in ordinary places among common folk. Each chapter is a story in itself, a jewel sparkling with wisdom. Strung together, the shimmering strand adorns simple truth: Life may be hard, but God is good. Detours happen by design. One way or another, the road leads home. So pay attention. Laugh. Wonder. And, sweet fancy Moses, don't forget to pick up the bread and milk."

—Jeanne Damoff, author of *Parting the Waters:
Finding Beauty in Brokenness*

"Author Billy Coffey weaves a poignant and poetic tale of a man rediscovering his faith and purpose. Told with charm and humor, SNOW DAY reveals how unexpected detours, 'chance' encounters, and everyday experiences lead to life's most valuable insights."

—Laura Cross, author, screenwriter, and writing coach

"I dare you to try walking away from Billy Coffey's words. He tells stories with the wit and energy of Mark Twain, albeit with compassion and spiritual vision. You won't regret that he reined you in, kept you sitting by the fire."

—L.L. Barkat, author of *Stone Crossings: Finding Grace in Hard and Hidden Places* and *Inside Out: poems*

"Everybody needs a snow day! To slow down and take a breath of what really is important."

—Don Mattingly, 1985 American League MVP

"Billy Coffey has created a town of winsome, appealing characters with strengths and struggles, faith and foibles—they're so realistic, I'm wishing I could pick up and move to that fictional town in Virginia in order to get to know them better. But the message of this novel is that no matter where we live, those people and their insights are all around us; meaningful stories are just waiting to be told. All we need to do is slow down enough to pay attention...all we need is one good snow day."

—Ann Kroeker, author of *Not So Fast: Slow-Down Solutions for Frenzied Families*

"With SNOW DAY, Billy offers further proof that the blogger-turned-author is a trend we've barely touched on. Honest, insightful, and packed with the writing people fell in love with online, SNOW DAY makes me proud to be a blogger."

—Jonathan Acuff, author of *Stuff Christians Like*

# SNOW DAY

A NOVEL

*Billy Coffey*

Faith
Words

New York   Boston   Nashville

FaithWords

Hachette Book Group

237 Park Avenue

New York, NY 10017

www.faithwords.com

Printed in the United States of America

First Edition: October 2010

10  9  8  7  6  5  4  3  2  1

FaithWords is a division of Hachette Book Group, Inc. The FaithWords name and logo are trademarks of Hachette Book Group, Inc.

Library of Congress Cataloging-in-Publication Data

Coffey, Billy.

Snow day / Billy Coffey.—1st ed.

p. cm.

Summary: "This poignant and gently humorous novel reveals how a completely ordinary day can change a whole life"—Provided by publisher.

ISBN 978-0-446-56826-5

1. Life change events—Fiction.  I. Title.

PS3603.O3165S66 2010

813'.6—dc22

2010001144

*For Allison, who once told me to put all my troubles in a box, sit on it, and laugh.*

# CONTENTS

# ACKNOWLEDGMENTS

The pages you're holding are the end result of a very long walk. Writing is like that, I think. It's a trek along a path through unknown wilderness that leaves you refreshed and satisfied, but also exhausted and hungry.

It can be a lonely walk. Not so much when you lift your head to smile at the sun, but certainly when you bow it to take the beating of a cold rain. Both are on that path, you know. There are hope and hopelessness, purpose and doubt. Which is why it always helps to have good company along the way.

My wife, Joanne, has been walking with me since the beginning. The words you're about to read would have been impossible to write without her.

Anne Lang Bundy was the one who found me near exhaustion and offered both a place to rest and a reason to keep going.

Rachelle Gardner calls herself my agent, but she's much more than that. Any trek through the wilderness is better with a guide to show you the way. She found me while I was lost, turned me around, and said, "Follow me." I'm glad I did. And still do.

To say that Kathy Richards made my walk easier would

not nearly be saying enough. She's led me through the dark places and shouldered much of my load. I can't thank her enough, but I'll keep trying.

Joey Paul, Holly Halverson, Whitney Luken, and the rest of the FaithWords family met me soon thereafter. They offered smiles and congratulations and more wisdom than I thought possible, then clapped me on the back and told me to keep walking.

That's just what I'm doing, which is fine with me. Because like I said, I have good company along the way.

# SNOW DAY

# 1

## *Bad Forecast*

Some things in life are constants. Mountains. Rivers. Sky.

But not on that particular December day.

A glimpse at the world from my bedroom window had become an essential part of waking up. I needed to face a new day with a sense of permanence in a world gone wobbly. I needed to know that the mountains hadn't roamed away during the night, the creek was right where I'd left it, and the sky hadn't fallen just yet. It reminded me that while some things changed, the best did not.

The sense of stability I relied upon evaporated that morning. A peek through the shade by my bed revealed a world more foreign than familiar. The sharp edges of my reality had been rubbed smooth by some unseen hand. The mountains had been uprooted and planted elsewhere, the creek had disappeared behind a wall of white, and the sky had indeed fallen.

"Sweet fancy Moses," I whispered.

"What's the matter?" my wife murmured, rolling over on an elbow to look at me. Abby pushed back the blond locks that a night's worth of sleep had drawn over her eyes. She laid a warm hand on my shoulder and countered the chill of the glass. The same hand that had held my own through weeks of countless prayers and long talks, the one she would slip around me as we lay in bed trying to keep together what was unraveling. I loved that hand.

"It's snowing," I said. "Hard. Gotta be six inches on the ground already."

Abby smiled. "Thought Frank said 'flurries.'"

Frank is the local channel 3 weatherman. Just eight hours earlier he had dispensed the standard ho-hum forecast for December in Virginia. "We have a thirty percent chance of scattered flurries overnight, with little or no accumulation. No worries, folks."

With his usual confidence and an ensemble of green screen maps, Doppler radar, barometric pressure readings, and Accu-Check surface temperatures, it had appeared he knew what he was talking about. But as I lifted the shade to get a clear view of the snow piling up in the yard, I became convinced that Frank's scientific approach to weather forecasting involved a call to his aunt in West Virginia, who stuck her head out the door and told him what was on the way.

I smiled. "Well, I guess he was right. There's just a few more flurries that are a little less scattered. No way you'll have school. Why don't you go back to bed?"

She yawned. "Check on the kids for me?"

"Sure thing," I said.

"Be careful going to work."

"I will."

"And call me right away if it happens."

"Okay."

"Promise?"

I looked away and pretended to be interested in the snow while I searched for an answer. Promise? I wasn't sure I could. "It" could happen that day or the next or the week after that. It had become so big and scary I wasn't sure I could call her right away if It came.

I patted her hand. "Don't worry, Abby," I said. "I'm not worried anymore."

I know it's bad to lie. But this was the sort of lie that if discovered would get me a peck on the jaw as forgiveness, which was good. It was a lie I needed to be the truth.

I showered and dressed, then took a right into the next room.

The Disney princess lamp on the bedside table had been left on in order to keep the monsters out and the angels in. The plan had worked, too. The soft light revealed no ogres and one cherub. Sara was still curled beneath the blankets. Her favorite stuffed bear sat at her left shoulder, keeping vigilant watch with its never-blinking eyes.

"Bye, baby doll," I whispered, kissing her forehead.

"The red flowers are the best," she offered. Commentary on the dream I couldn't enjoy with her.

"No doubt about it," I answered, then gave her bear a tap on the noggin.

In the bed next door, my son, Josh, had managed to flip himself over and upside down, leaving half his body exposed over the edge in a daring display of balance. His blue blanket still lay tucked into the back of his shirt, a leftover prop from our Superman story the night before.

I scooped him up and secured him under the blankets. When Sara was born, I was convinced the most difficult task for any father was to raise his daughter to be a woman. But then Josh came along and I knew better. I knew it was much harder to raise a boy to be a man. Especially when I considered the rocky road I had traveled to get there myself.

I leaned close. "Have a great day, little bear." I felt a *You, too, Dad* in blissful exhale.

I left his room and hesitated at the magical spot in the hallway where I could look into the sleeping faces of all three people who occupied the better part of my heart.

As a teacher, my wife would be given a needed day off. Time to rest and recuperate from a world of whiny students and screaming parents.

But if snow days were made for anyone, it was Sara and Josh. They were about to receive twelve hours of uncommon perfection, of snowmen and snowballs and vast amounts of hot chocolate. Their day would be experienced with the completeness and vigor known only to children. And then it would be tucked away into their tiny memories to be recalled whenever a happy thought was required. God had granted them an early Christmas present—one of the everlasting kind.

I left my family to their minivacation, poured a cup of coffee, and opened the living room curtains. The snowfall was closing in on the second porch step and would likely make it to the third within the hour. Ten inches by then. Maybe more.

"Just keeps piling up, doesn't it?" I asked no one. When no one answered, I shook my head in response.

How would Frank explain away a forecast drenched in science with a result less reliable than "Red sky at night, sailor's delight"? I turned on the television as I gathered my boots and coat. Various names of schools and businesses flashed on the bottom of the screen, announcing their closings for the day. In the top section a commercial played, promising worldly success and women aplenty if I switched my brand of deodorant.

I peered back into the white, trying to glimpse the outline of the Blue Ridge. I couldn't. My mountains were missing that day.

"Though the mountains be shaken and the hills removed, my unfailing love for you will not be shaken," I recited to Someone. I took another sip of coffee.

I watched the fluffy storm fall, smoothing the uneven places of our yard and turning the trodden pristine.

My life was once as pristine as the snow I watched. Clean and clear and light. Made such by the simple needs of a simple man who wanted little more from life than a family to love, a home we couldn't wait to get back to each afternoon, and a job that would keep us fed.

I figured I still had two out of the three, an average that would have me bound for Cooperstown if I played for the Yanks. That other third...that was the real storm I was peering into.

My life dictated my career. My education covered the essentials but little else. I didn't have any mechanical skills. I didn't own a farm. It all meant depending on the factory to provide my living.

The long-sputtering economy had finally found its way to Mattingly, leaving a lot of good people in a very bad place. Rumors had been spreading for weeks at work, fueled by a recent memo from management saying an exciting announcement was on its way. Their words, not mine. They even italicized it and put three exclamation points afterward—*Exciting Announcement!!!*

They didn't fool anybody. Exciting announcements and exclamation points meant good news to the average person, but in factoryspeak it meant you'd better start looking for another job. The union said layoffs were coming.

A thirty-four-year-old husband and father of two is at the place in life to be settling in, not starting over. A layoff would mean losing three-quarters of our income. With a mortgage, a vehicle payment, school loans, and no one hiring within thirty miles, the clouds began creeping in. Specters of worry and fear and dread. The gloom of a storm from which there seemed to be no escape.

The commercials ended and the news desk turned things over to Frank, now banished outside with parka and cameraman for some onsite reporting. I decided to cut him a break. Anyone can fail to see a storm coming. I had a bigger bad forecast to worry about.

So as Frank explained the hows and whys of the storm outside, I prayed about the one inside.

"What's happened to my life?" I asked.

("The storm just came out of nowhere, and it's now stalled over the mountains.")

"Tell me how to face this mess at work."

("—advising you to take extra precautions and be careful, because you're gonna need plenty of traction out there today.")

"I just don't know what to think right now."

("If you're able, you should be thinking about changing your plans.")

"I'm trying so hard to believe and trust, but I'm not sure how much longer I can hang on."

("—won't last long and I'm predicting sunshine in the afternoon.")

"—just want to know what You want me to do."

("So just gather yourself, hunker down, and call in well.")

I blinked through the window, lowered my coffee, and turned to face the television. Frank flashed me a knowing wink and handed things back over to the news desk.

*Huh*, I thought. *How about that?*

I pulled the cell phone from my pocket and left a message for my supervisor.

"Sammy," I said. "This is Peter. Put me down for an emergency vacation. I'm taking a snow day."

I snapped the phone shut and stared out at the porch, where the snow had just kissed the lip of the third step.

How was I supposed to face the storm at work? The same way Frank said to face the storm outside. I just needed to take some extra precautions. I had to gather myself up and hunker myself down. Be aware. Find traction.

Call in well.

# 2

## *Bread and Milk*

Abby stood beside me at the window and slipped her arm through mine. " 'Snow day,' huh?" she asked.

"Technically it's an 'emergency vacation.' I guess with everything going on, you could say this is an emergency."

"I'll say," she offered.

"Truth is, I couldn't bear the thought of the three of you having all the fun today." Then, more serious, "Besides, I could use the break. I need a little time to gather myself and hunker down."

"Everything has its reasons," Abby said. "Maybe you'll find some of your whys today."

"No doubt about it. And if there are any exciting announcements with exclamation points, Sammy will call."

"Well," she said, "what do you say we try and push all of that out of our minds for today? You get the kids up, and I'll start breakfast."

"Deal."

Getting two children aged five and three out of bed was rarely a battle. One nudge and one "Good morning" was sufficient to send both into kiddie hyperdrive. Children bring out some of the best emotions in their parents—those feelings of love and pride and joy. They also bring out some of the bad ones.

Sara and Josh stood in amazement at the snow outside, whipping themselves into a tiny but violent frenzy at the thought of spending their day in the wet and cold. By then I was ready to join them, too. But first there came another little matter to tend to.

"You have to go to the store," Abby said, walking back into the living room.

"I what?" I asked.

"You have to go to the store," she repeated.

"But I just took the day off. To be with my *family*. Going to the store by myself in the middle of a snowstorm is not being with my family, honey. Not even a little bit."

"I know," she agreed. "I really wouldn't ask, but we're low on a few things."

"What are we low on?" I asked.

"Bread and milk."

"We're low on bread and milk?"

"Yeah. And we'll need them."

"Why?"

"Because of the storm. You know everyone gets bread and milk in a storm."

I replied with my usual answer whenever I wanted to end a conversation with her that made no sense to me: "As you wish."

"And maybe a few more things, too," she said, already halfway back into the kitchen to root through the cabinets.

"Snow, Daddy, snow!" Josh said from the couch.

"I know, buddy. I just have to run to the store. Won't take me long, and we'll go out when I get back. Okay?"

"Okay, Daddy," he said, then resumed slurping juice from his sippy cup.

The "few more things" Abby had in mind turned out to be a list of about twenty items, many of which couldn't be found at the local grocery. Which left only one option.

"I think it's gotta be Super Mart," she said. She sweetened the words with a peck on the check, which brought a chuckle from Sara.

"Super Mart? Really?"

"Shouldn't take you too long."

Another peck. Another chuckle from the little girl on the couch.

"But I'll have to take the detour," I said.

"It'll give you time to think. You know, gather yourself and hunker down?"

"Stupid weatherman," I mumbled.

Ten minutes later I was slogging down what I could only assume was the road out of our neighborhood. The snowplows were still hours away from reaching the back roads, so I was forced to estimate where the going side of the road began and where the coming side ended. With the blowing snow and my tired eyes, I had to squint just to make sure I wasn't taking a shortcut through someone's backyard.

I pulled over at the gray Cape Cod near the end of the street. In the driveway was a petite lady bundled in a ski coat that looked three sizes too large. Perched on the front tire of her Jeep, she waved a broom back and forth along the windshield, scraping away a night's worth of flurries.

"Mornin', Mandy," I called, rolling down my window.

She pushed the toboggan cap up from her eyes and waved a gloved hand. "Hey, Peter. How are you?"

"Fair," I said. "Yourself?"

"Oh, I'm good. Just trying to get all this mess off my vehicle. Don't see how you people manage to survive between November and March."

I laughed. "You'll get used to it again."

"I suppose," she said, jumping from the tire and walking my way. "I've gotten used to everything else. Might as well get used to winter again, too."

"I didn't think you'd be heading for work," I said. Mandy was the secretary for a local surveying company. Since there was so much snow on the ground, I figured there wouldn't be much call for surveying that day.

"Davey already called and said I had the day off. You?"

"Snow day. Figured I deserved a break."

"I'm sure. Heard anything yet?"

Like most people in town, Mandy had kept up with the news about the factory.

"Nope. Knowing them, they'll probably tell us Christmas Eve."

"Well, don't you worry. Sometimes God lets us hurt a while so He can show us what really matters in life."

"I suppose," I said. "Where you going if you don't have to go to work?"

"Oh, I was just getting Jack ready to go to the store. Need some bread and milk, you know. Because of the storm? I haven't forgotten that."

Bread and milk again. Because of the storm again.

"Well, I'm on my way to Super Mart," I said. "No sense in you and little Jack going out. How about I pick you up some and drop it by on my way back?"

"Oh, thank you. That'd be great. Not much snow down in Arizona, you know. It's pretty to look at, but I'm not crazy about driving around in it. Especially with the detour and all."

"No problem. I'll see you later," I said, rolling up my window and waving.

The drive to Super Mart took much longer than usual, and it didn't have anything to do with the weather. The Department of Transportation had decided that the road connecting our neighborhood to town was a flooding hazard. No big deal, they said. Shouldn't take more than a week.

By the day of the storm, it had been a month.

Though our neighborhood consisted of people who lived by the easy-does-it mentality of country life, our patience was wearing thin. The detour set up to keep drivers away from the repair added at least twenty minutes for any trip into town and had become yet another blight on my once shiny life. I hated that detour.

But there is a bright side to everything, and on that day the detour provided me a little time to ponder what I was doing and why.

Abby was right. When a bad storm hit, everyone around here stocked up on bread and milk. There wasn't a loaf of bread left in the entire county during the snowstorm of '96, and two old ladies literally came to blows in Food King over the last gallon of Shenandoah's Pride. Saw it with my own eyes. It took three people to pull them apart. They knocked over a display of bottled water and four cases of soda in the process.

The excesses of modern times are tempered when the weather rages, reducing us to our primal selves. We are highly advanced, twenty-first-century people. We have computers and cell phones and combustible engines. But dump a foot of snow on the ground and suddenly we think we're in an episode of *Little House on the Prairie*. This is especially true when it comes to provisions. We have in our kitchens enough nourishment to last weeks—bananas from South America, fish from Alaska, beef from Texas, oranges from Florida. The bounty of the world lies no more than a few steps from our living room. And I was sure Mandy's pantry was similarly stocked. And yet there I was driving all the way into town for bread and milk.

Why?

Jimmy Buffett had just begun another song about warm breezes and sunny beaches when my thoughts settled on Mandy.

She and Jack had come to the neighborhood alone. Transplants from the Grand Canyon State. Not too many people move to Virginia from Arizona. More often it was the other way around. A fact I had mentioned to her shortly after they had moved in.

"I'm not moving as much as I'm running," she replied. She clarified that it wasn't so much what she was running from as what she was running toward.

Home.

Mandy had been born and raised in a small house near the railroad tracks not too far from where she'd been standing. The wrong side of the tracks, mind you. At eighteen, she decided to follow her bliss over the mountains to Arizona State, where she met the love of her life in a lawyer whose wealth was transcended only by his violence. Mandy endured under the false assumptions that an abusive husband wouldn't necessarily become an abusive father and that the comfort in her life was worth the pain in her marriage. When he raised a hand to Jack in a drunken rage, she took their son and left. In the end, she found that the very mountains she always thought had kept her hemmed in now protected her and Jack from their past.

It hadn't been easy for her. Mandy confessed to Abby that there were times when the bills were paid late and the money was short and she wondered if she'd really made the right choice. But those were the times when she would look at her son and her God and see just how better off she was.

She doesn't have the stuff anymore—the fancy cars and big houses and high teas with the country club wives. And that's okay, because the stuff never made her happy anyway. Mandy didn't need a rich life of fine wine and filet mignon. Not when a simple life of bread and milk would be better. She had weathered her storm by finding the constants of her life. She had people to love, a God to lean on, and a reason to face every day. How could any dream be better than that?

I realized then the real reason I'd taken off work. I needed to search for my constants. For my own bread and milk of my life that would sustain me if life at work unraveled.

So as I drove I prayed for what Mandy had. I asked God to help me believe that if I lost what means much, it would be so I could find what means more.

# 3

---- ❄ ----

## *The Superman Costume*

There were those in this world who possessed the economic wherewithal to avoid the experience of having to shop at Super Mart. I was not among them. Ambivalence was not generally a part of my personality. I loved some things, loathed some others, but rarely did the two emotions converge on one point. Super Mart was one of those points.

The parking lot was just as busy as usual. Not even the snowstorm could keep people away from a deal on detergent and 10W-30 motor oil. I found a spot about a mile and a half away from the entrance. The snow fell so fast and the store itself was so far away that I found myself praying for God to send me a Sherpa so I wouldn't get lost.

After what seemed like an hour's walk, the doors appeared through the blowing snow and slid open. On the other side I was met by an elderly man wearing so many layers of clothing that his arms were trapped in a *T*, as if he were preparing to dive into deep water. There was a layer of snow and ice on his beard and a What-did-I-do-to-deserve-this look on his face, but that didn't stop him from offering me a good morning and a shopping cart. I took both.

I glanced at Abby's shopping list. "Stocking stuffers."

As I approached them, I could see Super Mart's toy aisles were even busier than the grocery section on the other side of the store appeared to be, in spite of the fact that the day's events required more in the way of practical shopping than indulgence. The seven aisles of baby dolls and action figures and whatnot were just a step or two below a brawl. Particularly the girls' section.

I rolled my shopping cart around the outside of the girls' aisles, waiting for an opening. After five trips, I still hadn't found one. I decided then that Sara had been pretty well taken care of as far as presents went. It was a selfish notion, and I knew it, but the thought of wading through a crowd of apprehensive, stressed-out mothers made me a little squeamish. I would concentrate on Josh's stocking stuffers instead. The boys' section of toys seemed a little less congested and a little more civil.

It's tough to find toys for a three-year-old. Josh was too old for rattles and the teething toys, but too young for action figures and Hot Wheels. There wasn't much in the middle.

Inspiration struck when I spotted the rack of Superman toys. Little boys love Superman, and my little boy was no exception. Everything you could have ever wanted in a Superman toy was hanging on those racks. Action figures, play sets, games. The trick was going to be picking out which to buy.

A quick look at the "4+" on the action figures told me they would not do. Which meant the play sets would not do, either, since a play set without an action figure was basically just a clump of plastic. And the games? Josh hadn't even mastered Candyland yet. This was tragic.

It looked as though my son would have to endure one more year of stuffed animals and those big, fluffy baby books.

But hanging beside the action figures were a collection of Superman costumes: tights, cape, and shirt (complete with fake abdominal muscles) for a little over ten dollars. A bargain if I had ever seen one. It was the perfect gift. And there was even one left in Josh's size—extra runt.

Ten dollars was a little too expensive for a stocking stuffer, especially in light of the seven-dollar maximum Abby and I had agreed upon. Still, it was a Superman costume. A *real* one. Much better than the red T-shirt, bath towel, and safety pin I had to use when I was his age.

I snatched it from the rack before anyone else hovering around me could. I checked the quality (marginal, but satisfactory), the durability (knowing Josh, I gave it a life span of about two weeks before he either grew out of it or ripped holes in it to mimic bullet holes), and the kid factor (Superman was daily DVD viewing for my son).

Then I made one last but crucial check, which was to see if my wife could throw the suit into the washing machine without its falling apart like a wet tissue. The front of the tag didn't say, so I flipped it over to see if the washing instructions had been printed there. They hadn't. Instead, printed was a warning.

"Caution," the label said in bold black letters. "Wearing this costume will not enable you to fly."

I read it twice and burst out laughing. The shoppers around me glanced my way and then began to quietly disperse, no doubt believing that the poor man beside them had just snapped under the pressure of the storm and the season. I offered to show the tag to a gentleman standing beside me. He gave me a quick smile, held up his hands, and backed away.

Why in the world would such a warning need to be put on a costume? Sure, companies put warning labels on their products to cover themselves against any legal ramifications due to their buyers' idiocy. But the warning couldn't have been for the child; all the sizes were so small that whoever was wearing it would surely not be old enough to read. And even if they could, what kid reads the tags on his clothes?

This left the parents. That was a sad consideration. For some reason the company thought it at least somewhat likely that some parents would buy their Superman costumes and tell their kids to put them on and go jump off the roof.

Ridiculous.

As if grown people thought that wearing a superhero outfit could turn you into one. Could make you fly, even. As if people thought that becoming Superman was a rather plausible reality.

Then again, I thought, maybe it wasn't so ridiculous after all.

My father wanted to be Superman when he was a kid. Me, too. And from the look of things thus far, my son was well on his way to carrying on not only our family tradition, but the family tradition for millions. It seemed to me that every guy in America wanted to be Superman at some point in his life.

And who could blame us? Being able to fly faster than a speeding bullet, more powerful than a locomotive, and able to leap tall buildings in a single bound had its advantages. Not to mention the whole heat vision thing and the fact that Superman could reverse time.

Superman could do anything.

So we indulged our fantasies, flying around our homes with bath towels safety-pinned around our necks, fighting for truth, justice, and the American way—defeating evil through power and sheer will.

Playing superhero didn't last, though. Whether he likes it or not, at some point every boy must become a man. Life's truths must be redefined from soft to hard. We realized that not every story ended happily ever after, not every cloud had a silver lining, and superheroes were just cartoons to pass the time. If Superman were real, he'd end up like every other man. He'd grow old and screw up and his hair would start falling out. His back would hurt from a day's work, and he would develop an audible grunt whenever he bent over to pick something up off the floor.

Of the entire Superman myth, only the kryptonite seemed real. It wasn't a green rock from some far-flung planet, though. Adults' kryptonite became the ticking of our days, the slow yet inevitable forward motion of time.

A few, however, resisted. Some kept right on playing their own version of superhero, tweaked to correspond with just enough reality to keep them off the psychiatrist's couch. They faced life with chests puffed and chins out, impervious to the pain that lurks both in this moment and the next. Standing tall against adversity. Fighting for happiness and peace and the American dream.

It was a lie, this life.

I should know. I was living it.

The stone wall I had erected between my life and my job was a mere façade, made more of sand than stone. I worried and fretted. I was afraid. Yet I tried to keep all of these things hidden from family and friends for this one simple reason: I was a man, and men didn't feel such things.

As long as I kept that costume on, I knew I was safe. I could fly. It wasn't until I pondered that warning label that I realized I wasn't soaring through my hardship, I was falling.

Faster than a speeding bullet? Hardly. I couldn't even outrun my life. More powerful than a locomotive? I'd found many things that were much bigger and much badder than I. And as for leaping tall buildings in a single bound, I knew then that the mountains we all had to climb in life required more than one step.

Standing there in the middle of Super Mart, I had an epiphany: I had to take off my costume, because I wasn't Superman.

And I knew this as well: one day my son would have to make that same decision. But he would also discover that the God in heaven he prayed to at night was also inside of him. And that the God who lived in his heart could allow him to do some amazing things in this life. Maybe nothing as fabulous as heat vision. But something more practical, like seeing the truth of things. He wouldn't be able to lift cars, but he would be able to lift spirits. He wouldn't be faster than a speeding bullet, but he would be able to take the shots life dished out and stand up again.

I placed the outfit in my cart, satisfied that I could cross one more item off the list. But before I wheeled on I reached back down, tore the warning label off, then put it into my pocket. Josh could have the costume for Christmas. I'd give him the label when he got older.

# 4

## *Beautiful Scars*

Zigzagging my cart through the aisles and around people, I slowed my steps and quickened my senses to take in the surroundings. The place was alive with activity. The festivity of the season was awash in fake Christmas trees and rows of candy canes and enough wrapping paper to cover the entire eastern seaboard.

The bread section was immediately to my right, easily spotted by the crowd of people attacking it. Shopping carts were slammed into one another. Tempers were beginning to flare. Children were screaming. The loudspeakers were trying to soothe the stressed-out shoppers with Bing Crosby's "White Christmas," but the scene in front of me was more *Apocalypse Now.* A bag of hot dog buns flew through the air, only to be snatched up by two hungry hands. I then knew I had been recruited for a suicide mission. I would never get out of there alive.

But like any good soldier, I intended to carry out my orders. I left my cart, sure that it would not be there when I got back—if I got back—and flung myself into the throng. I came out with the last loaf of butter bread, raising it above my head like the spoils of war. Then I remembered that I had to get a loaf for Mandy and Jack as well. I briefly considered just cutting the one I had in half, for surely that would be enough to get everyone through the day. But I had promised a loaf. I dove back in. By some act of Christmas magic, I had two loaves in my hand when I came out. And my cart was even where I'd left it.

Deciding to press my luck a bit, I rolled down to the milk coolers, where by some miracle the crowd was not only small but almost civil.

That was when I saw it. Perched atop the nether regions of the closeout shelves like a gargoyle, ugly keeping worse ugliness away.

If the fears and worries of my life could have somehow been fashioned into a physical representation, the end result would have looked much like the figurine that was in front of me. The Santa was just that awful. And the more it repulsed me, the more I couldn't look away.

Jolly Saint Nick wasn't so jolly. He was tired. His rosy cheeks were a pallid gray, almost brown. And the toy sack he carried wasn't really a sack as much as it was a small clump of mashed black dangling from his right hand. His smile was more of an I-hate-this-time-of-year frown, as if Christmas Eve was about as fun as having a stick thrust into his eye. Part of his nose had been chipped off by some previous fall or drop. I picked him up. On the bottom of his cardboard container was a sticker that said, "Pres Santa's belly to hear him talk!" Yes—"Pres." I did. What came out of his mouth wasn't "Ho, Ho, Ho!" or "Merry Christmas!" It was more like "Clarrmm homba dwee!"

No wonder it had been banished to Super Mart's version of the Island of Misfit Toys. Where in the world did they get that thing? And who in their right mind would ever plop down—I looked at the sticker price—*three dollars* for such a piece of junk?

I shook my head in wonder and put the Santa back on the shelf where it belonged. Still staring, I pushed my cart blindly out into the aisle.

And collided with the people coming around the corner.

Elderly couple. With a cart full of bread and milk and a couple of DVDs.

"I am so sorry," I said, backing my cart away from theirs.

"No problem," the man said, doing the same. "Sometimes we come here just to play a little bumper buggies and get our frustrations out."

"You two picked the right day, then."

"Is it still snowing outside?" the woman with him asked.

"Afraid so."

"Afraid so?" she asked. "Now what's that kind of talk? I think it's wonderful."

"I'm a spring-and-summer kind of guy myself," I said. I looked up from my cart long enough to notice that the left side of her face had been badly scarred by a long-ago burn. I averted my eyes and smiled.

"My apologies again," I said. "You two have a nice day."

"Merry Christmas," the woman said with a smile.

I strolled off and glanced back at the couple as I rounded the corner. Both were parked right in front of the sick Santa that had grabbed my attention. I stopped to watch, amused that they, too, were playing the role of curious pedestrians.

The woman had taken the Santa off the shelf where I had left it. The man gawked at it and pushed Santa's belly. The sound came out even more garbled than before. They both laughed and shook their heads with the same sort of wonder I had felt. But instead of putting the figure back onto the shelf and moving on, he placed it in their cart.

Curiosity gripped me. Though I had spoken with them only briefly, I could tell they were two intelligent people. They were well-dressed and competent. They had opted for the more expensive milk and the fancier brand of bread. Their choice of DVDs led me to believe they preferred high-brow to low-brow. These were not two dummies. At least, not until they picked up the Santa and put it in their cart.

I pushed my buggy back over to them.

"Excuse me," I said.

"Hello again," said the woman.

"Back for more bumper buggies?" the man asked.

"No, no, I've had enough of that." I paused, unsure of how to broach the subject. "I was just wondering about that Santa. I was looking at it before our run-in."

"Oh," he said, reaching into their cart. "You didn't want it—"

"No-no-no," I said, waving my arms and trying to keep the thing as far away from me as possible. "No, I don't want it. I just wanted to know why *you* want it."

"Pardon?" the woman asked.

"I'm a curious kind of guy," I explained. "Always asking questions and whatnot. Drives my wife crazy, but she's not here. Would you indulge me?"

She reached into their cart and retrieved the Santa. The two of them examined it a bit. She smiled. "It's pretty," she said.

Pretty.

"Oh come on," I said. "That's the worst excuse for a Santa I've ever seen in my life. That thing is ugly."

"Don't think so," the man said. "Don't think so at all. It has…what's the word, Helen?"

"Character," Helen offered.

"Yes. Yes, that's the word. That Santa has *character*. Rather beautiful, I would say."

So now the monstrosity wasn't just pretty. It was beautiful, too.

"Sorry folks, and all due respect, but you two are nuts."

"Well, it wouldn't be the first time we've been accused of being that," Helen said, smiling.

"Here," the man offered, "take a good look at him. Sure, this Santa's not as nice as the ones over there on aisle twelve. I mean after all, he's stuck over here on the closeout aisle for a reason, right? But that doesn't make him any less valuable."

"No," I said. "But what *does* make him less valuable is his condition."

"His condition?" Helen asked.

"Yes. He's broken. Busted. Worthless." I ran out of synonyms.

"But look at what the poor fella's been through," the man said. "Banged and dropped and who knows what else. But he's still trying, isn't he? He's still *around*. Still useful."

"He's ugly," I restated.

Helen said, "And do you think that because he is scarred he is not useful?"

I sensed a trap. Both Helen and her husband were sporting Cheshire smiles. "Well," I said, weighing my words carefully, "yes. Yes, *that* Santa is useless because *it* is scarred."

They both beamed. The trap had been sprung. They knew it, and I knew it. But I was still curious.

"About forty years ago," Helen began, "I was in an accident. The doctors said it was a miracle that I survived. Doctors back then were more willing to throw that word out there than they are now. But they said it, and they meant it. I wasn't supposed to live, but I did. I was grateful, too. But the only problem was this."

She pointed to her face. I looked down a bit when she did, but she would have none of it.

"Oh come now, no reason for that. I know you noticed it, and that's fine. I mean, who *wouldn't* notice it? Still, it looks better now than it did back then. Back then, it was so horrible that I refused to leave my apartment. I was in college at the time, but I dropped out. I couldn't bear the thought of going to class and having people see me."

"That must have been awful," I offered.

"Oh, it was. I got by, though. My parents helped me out moneywise, and back then the grocery store always had some schoolchildren who would deliver groceries to me. I would always tape the money to the door. They would leave the groceries there, and no one would be the wiser.

"But cutting myself off from the world became even more painful than my accident. I was tired of being lonely. So one day I got out of bed and decided I was going to do something about it. It was raining outside, and I decided to go to the park for a walk. There wouldn't be anyone there in the rain. I thought it would be a good first step.

"I took a loaf of bread and walked to the duck pond. Found a nice bench that was kind of off to itself. Just in case, you know, someone came by. When I pulled out my bag of bread, it fell onto the ground. I bent down to pick it up, but it was in someone's hand."

"It was in my hand," her husband said.

Helen looked at him and smiled, and then she looked at me. "Yes, it was in Charlie's hand. I jerked up, and in my surprise I looked straight at him. I didn't know what to do. I was simply mortified."

"I saw her face," Charlie said. "And she knew it. I was surprised by it, of course, and I think for a moment she saw that on my face."

"I did," Helen confessed. "All I wanted to do was run away. But then Charlie did something I would have never expected. He *smiled* at me. Such a simple gesture done every day by people everywhere, but it meant so much. He saw my scars, but he also saw *me*."

"What'd you say?" I asked Charlie.

"Nothing at first. And then I mumbled a simple hello. I told her it was a beautiful day to be out at the park, which got a little chuckle out of her. I was just as shy as she was. Scared to death, too."

"He had his reasons," Helen said. "It didn't take me long to find out."

"What do you mean?" I asked.

"Well, we talked for a little while. It was just small talk, really—normal, everyday things. But to me it seemed like the first conversation I'd ever had. Charlie was such a nice young man, and I had missed the company of a gentleman in my life. I could tell he was just as apprehensive as I was, but I thought it was just because of my face. He didn't want to seem rude, so he couldn't just leave. Finally, I decided to let him off the hook. I told him I was late for an appointment. He said that he was glad to meet me and even asked for my telephone number."

"Quite a bold gesture in those days," he said.

"It was a *sweet* gesture," she corrected. "But I knew nothing would come of it. I gave it to him, though, and then I left. I walked away. But Charlie just stood there, staring at me. I felt so embarrassed. I could just imagine him going back to wherever he came from and telling everyone about the freak he met at the park. I started to cry. I was going back to my apartment and never coming out again.

"Then I realized I had left my purse back on that park bench. Charlie never noticed it, and in the throes of our conversation I had forgotten all about it. Everything was in there, too—you know how women are with their purses. I didn't have a choice but to go back. When I got there, I saw Charlie was walking away. And I realized why he had been staring at me before. He wasn't appalled by my face. He was just watching to make sure I was out of sight before he left."

"Why?" I asked them both.

Helen smiled. "Because Charlie was limping."

Charlie took a hand off the shopping cart and knocked on his right leg. "World War Two," he said. "Grenade got me in the knee."

"Wow," I managed to say. "I'm sorry."

"Sorry?" he said. "Son, don't apologize to me. It was my duty and I did it. And more than that, I was glad to do it. I got this back in 'forty-three. I was pretty banged up. Most of my friends were either still in the war or already dead. And there I was, just a crippled boy of nineteen. The docs said they could fix me up mostly, but there wasn't much they could do about this.

"I was a proud boy. Real athletic. But all of a sudden it took me more time to walk out to the mailbox than it used to take to leg out a triple. It was hard on me, you know?"

"I bet," I answered.

"I pouted for a long while. Thought my life was over. I was a cripple, and who'd want a cripple? I'd never meet anyone, never have a family, never get to do anything. I figured I'd end up dying an old, lonely man in the very bedroom I grew up in."

"What changed your mind?" I asked.

"I decided to take a walk one day. Not the day I met Helen—that came later. But I just realized that even though God let things get bad, that didn't mean He intended for them to stay that way. I had to do something to show Him I was still trying, that I still had faith.

"So I just started walking around the park. It took me forever, and it hurt, but I loved it. Couldn't get enough of it. I walked every day, rain or shine. About a month later, I met Helen."

"It wasn't easy for us," Helen said. "Not at first. We were both so afraid. We both felt like sooner or later the other would wake up and decide there was sure to be someone better somewhere out there."

"But that never happened, did it?" I asked.

"No," Charlie said. "I love her. I loved her from the first moment we met. I know that sounds silly, but it's true. Love at first sight?" He raised his eyebrows. "It's real. I'm telling you it's real. I love her." He paused to look at his bride. "I love her because she's beautiful."

"You stop being so fresh in front of strangers," Helen teased.

He winked at his wife, and she smiled back. Then a sale on a set of tools caught Charlie's eye in the next aisle. He excused himself and walked over to take a better look.

Helen and I watched him leave, and as he did I noticed that his right leg dragged slightly behind his left. Like his wife, Charlie had to endure the consequences of fate for the rest of his life. Some consequences are like that. The pain may be temporary, but the reminder is forever. That didn't mean life couldn't still be beautiful.

Helen touched my arm. I looked over at her and she whispered, "Charlie's right, you know."

"About what?" I asked.

"About me being beautiful. Charlie told me once that my scars made me beautiful, that if I hadn't gone through all of that, then God couldn't have made me the person I am."

She smiled her Cheshire smile again. I looked down at the sick Santa in her buggy, and I smiled, too.

Helen and Charlie fell in love when they both felt as though no one could possibly love them. They fell in love because each knew the other would understand their struggles and their pain. Perhaps they both felt the Santa was some sort of symbol for their lives. Yes, he was beaten and battered and scarred, but that didn't mean he was worthless.

And what about me? I paused and reflected upon even the small part of my life that I could remember, and I saw a lot of scars. I had done plenty of things of which I wasn't proud. Harmful things. Hurtful things. Things I wished I could take back but couldn't. Helen carried her scars on the outside, but mine were on the inside. And I would argue they were much worse. But there was a God who still loved me, who sent His very Son to die for me. Little, rotten, scarred me.

Was it love? Yes, I was sure it was. But it was also the fact that He saw past all of those scars to some beauty inside of me that I had yet to find. And, perhaps, never would.

"I think I understand," I said.

"Good. Well, I'll be going. Charlie gets lost over there in the tool section. It's a man thing, you know."

"Yes ma'am, I know."

"You have a good day now. And mind the snow on the way home."

"I will," I said. "And you, too."

Helen began wheeling her cart away, then turned around, picking up the Santa and nodding at me.

I nodded back.

# 5

———✳———

## *Passing It On*

I had been following him for a few minutes. Older man, gray hair, and very nosy.

I remembered seeing him as I was trying to find my way into Super Mart through the snow and abandoned shopping carts. Parked in a white Chevy Silverado about midway to the store. Just sitting there, engine off, sipping some coffee. I also remembered wondering why someone would drive all the way out to Super Mart in a snowstorm just to sit in the parking lot and sip some coffee.

An old Ford LTD crawled into a parking space near him as I walked past, and we both watched as a family of three got out and made their way toward the store. Mother, father, and a son about six. Mother was wearing a pair of faded jeans and a ragged blue sweater that was covered by an even more ragged parka. Father was dressed in what was known in Mattingly as "weekly wear"—overalls and a flannel shirt. A John

Deere cap was pulled down over his long hair. The son was in sweatpants and a sweatshirt, both of which were badly stained and a size or two bigger than necessary.

In other words, they were poor. We try our best to dress up the economic condition of that portion of society. We call them "disadvantaged" or "lower class" or a myriad of other euphemisms, mostly to lessen the guilt that they exist. But they do and they are poor and there's just no way to make it sound any better.

The other man, I noticed, got out of his truck and followed them into the store. It was a strange sight, almost as if he was waiting for them. It got my interest up enough to follow him as he followed them. But then we all got into the store and I became more concerned with my shopping list, then met Helen and Charlie, and then, well, I just forgot.

But I remembered again when I saw the little boy, tugging on his mother's shirt and begging to visit the toys that taunted him from across the aisle. It was an old trick used by both children and husbands when attempting to gain permission from the women in their lives—when you can't convince them, wear them down.

It worked, too. Because a few more minutes and tugs later, his mother said, "Just *go*, Jacob. But stay where we can see you."

So Jacob went. And so did I.

Standing to one side of the aisle, Jacob would pick up every toy he could reach without regard to make or model, turning it around in his tiny hands and scrutinizing every detail. He would then gently place the toy back on the shelf, pick up the next, and repeat.

I looked around. Mother and father were nowhere to be

found. Spooky Gray Man, however, was. He stood at the end of the aisle, peeking around the corner at the boy.

As a father of two small children, I tend to be a little protective when it comes to kids. With his mother and father off in parts unknown and Spooky Gray Man eyeing their son, my hero complex kicked in. I was going to watch him watch.

The little boy made his way from the Legos over to the Tonka trucks. That's where he stopped, right in front of a bright green and yellow John Deere tractor. Spooky Gray Man was about ten feet away, craning his neck around a lady who was busy surveying the G.I. Joes. I was standing about ten feet farther back, trying to decide if I was going to hit him in the throat or the jaw when he tried to snatch the boy. Not kidding.

The boy picked up the tractor. His eyes bulged as he turned the box over and then back again. He ran a hand down the side, feeling the soft coolness of the metal. Yes, *metal*. This was no cheapo toy. This was the real thing, complete with rubber tires and a genuine farmer action figure with blue jeans and flannel shirt. Meant not for carpets and hardwood floors, but for the sand and the mud.

Spooky Gray Man excused himself around the lady in his way to get a better look, though I wasn't sure if it was a better look at the tractor or the boy. I took a couple of steps forward myself.

It was just then that the mother and father showed up. Spooky Gray Man took a few steps back and feigned attention at a Noah's ark puzzle.

"Daddy, look!" the boy said, holding up the prize for his father's approval. "It's just like the one you drive!"

"Yep, sure is," the father answered. "Sure is a nice one."

"Do you think Santa could bring me this, Daddy? Huh?"

His mother looked down and peered at the price. I didn't know how much it was, but from the look on her face, *too much* would suffice. She looked at her husband and shook her head.

"Well, maybe," he said. "But you already sent off your letter. I don't know if he'd get another one in time for Christmas Eve."

"But I'd be extra good, Daddy. *Extra*. I promise."

"I know, sweetie," his mother said, trying to find a good excuse. "But that sure is a big toy, and I don't know if Santa could fit it into his bag without having to take some other little boy's present out."

*Not bad*, I nodded.

"Then another little boy might not get any presents?" he asked.

"That's right," the father said, obviously pained that he had to say it.

This was a good kid, made evident by the fact that the explanation stumped him. He ran a hand down the side of the tractor again. His bottom lip quivered for a bit, but held steadfast. "Okay," he finally mumbled. "But maybe Santa will bring me one anyway, right, Daddy?"

Daddy knew better. Daddy knew who Santa really was. And Daddy knew Santa simply didn't have the cash.

"I don't know, son. Maybe. But maybe you'll just have to wait a while for that one."

"You'll see," the boy smiled. "Santa will bring it. You'll see, Daddy."

The two parents exchanged a quick look, and there was

a shared sigh. For a lot of families, Christmas was the best time of the year. For others, it was just another day that their children would have to go without.

They each extended a hand to their son, who took one in each of his, and together they made their way out of the toy section. Spooky Gray Man followed, obviously not ready to give up just yet.

I followed, too, me right behind him and him right behind them. It was an odd sight to say the least, but I tried to appear as innocent as I could. I wasn't in a hurry. This was no longer a matter of protecting an innocent child. Mom and Dad could do that. I was just plain nosy.

The family settled in the frozen food aisle of the grocery section. Spooky Gray Man watched as they filled their shopping cart with two-for-one frozen pizzas. When they wheeled over to the canned goods, though, Spooky Gray Man didn't follow. Instead he went the opposite way, back toward the other side of the store. Puzzled, I decided to follow.

When he again stopped at the toys, I first thought he was trying to find another child, at which point I was going to put a swift end to the whole thing. But instead he did something that both astonished and puzzled me. Spooky Gray Man headed straight for the John Deere tractor Jacob had held, picked it up, and walked off toward the cash registers.

I followed and watched as he wormed his way through the crowd to a checkout line, paid for the toy, and left.

*What is this guy doing?* I asked myself. *Is he taking a souvenir? Buying it for his own grandson? Or is he just plain screwed up in the head?*

I hid my cart behind a Pepsi display and prayed to God that He'd send an angel to protect the goods inside. Then I buttoned my coat and followed him as he walked out of the store. It was time for the truth. I was just going to come right out and ask him what he was up to.

Spooky Gray Man stopped at the old Ford LTD and brushed the snow away from the driver's side window. The door was of course unlocked. There was nothing inside worth stealing.

He pulled a small notebook from his pocket, scribbled a note, and placed the note and the toy in the backseat. He then shut the door, walked over to his own vehicle, and resumed sipping his coffee.

I retraced my steps and situated myself next to the entrance, where I could see both the people coming in and out of the store and Spooky Gray Man's truck. After a bit Jacob and his family came out, their shopping cart full of the week's provisions. I peered through the snow at the man in the truck. He had straightened himself in his seat and eyed the family.

Mother and father reached the car and began loading the groceries into the trunk. Jacob ambled through the snow and into the backseat. For a moment, there was silence. Then came the scream, high-pitched and long.

His parents came running. They didn't know why or what had happened, but I imagine they fully expected to see blood. Jacob, however, was fine. More than fine. He was *ecstatic*. He slipped out of the backseat and into the parking lot, then thrust the toy in their faces, yelling and screaming and jumping up and down. "It's real!" he screamed, "it's really real!" Then, as if the gravity of the situation had just struck him, he jerked his head up into the falling snow, hoping to see the last vestiges of reindeer hooves.

Jacob didn't see Santa. He was looking in the wrong direction. But I saw him. He wasn't flying off into the gray sky shouting, "Merry Christmas to all, and to all a good night!" He was pulling out of the Super Mart parking lot in a white Chevrolet truck.

Mother and father didn't know what to do. At first, I supposed, they considered the possibility that their son had pilfered it from the store. But how? Where could he have hidden it?

Then the father saw the note.

He mouthed the written words and then looked around the parking lot. Everything looked to be the normal commotion of people going about their own lives. Not a Santa to be seen. He tilted the page to his wife, who read it with a hand over her mouth. When she finished, she and her husband looked at one another for a long while.

He tucked the note into his pocket and finished loading the groceries. Jacob's mother walked over and grabbed him up, putting both him and his new present into the backseat. As the father shut the trunk, he reached into his pocket and read the note again.

There was only one thing on my mind right then. I had to know what that note said.

I walked over to him and said, "Hey, buddy."

"How ya doin'?" the father answered.

"Good. Don't think this snow's gonna stop anytime soon, though."

"Nope," he said. "Don't reckon it will."

We stood there as an awkward silence grew. "I heard your little boy. Sounded like he was pretty excited about something."

"Yeah," he said. "He sure was. Christmas present, you know."

"Oh yeah? You couldn't keep that one until Christmas morning, huh?"

"Shoot," he answered, "it wasn't ours to keep. Somebody just stuck it in the car. Wife and I just couldn't believe it."

"Huh," I said. "That's a little strange, isn't it?"

"Buddy, you don't know the strange part."

"Oh yeah?" I prodded.

"It was one of them John Deere tractors. You know, the real kind? My boy wanted that thing real bad. *Real* bad. But the thing's thirty bucks, you know?"

"Pretty steep."

"You ain't kiddin'. I mean, I work hard, you know. But…" he trailed off, then glanced at his family waiting in the car. "But we ain't got much."

I looked at his family. His wife was turned around in her seat smiling at Jacob, who was beaming with joy in the back-seat. Yes, they may not have had much in the way of money, but they had a lot in the way of love. Financial security is one thing. Family security is quite another. Love can get you through a lot more than money can.

"Looks like you have a lot to me," I said.

He smiled. "Yep, we got each other. That's all I need. I want to give my son more, you know? But that toy? Just too expensive." He shook his head for emphasis. "We didn't have the heart to tell him. So my wife said that maybe Santa didn't have enough room in his sleigh. I know that's bad," he said, before I could say that it wasn't, "but what else are we gonna say? 'Sorry, son, we're just too poor'? I don't think so.

"So we get out here and the thing is just sittin' there in the backseat. Just *sittin'* there, like it fell straight outta heaven. And then there was this."

He handed me the note, and I opened it. Written in blue ink was this:

God gave to me, and now I give to you.
Merry Christmas.
Pass it on.

"Man," I said. "That's something."

"You bet it is. And I tell you what, whoever did that didn't just make my boy's Christmas. He made his mom and dad's Christmas, too."

We said our good-byes and I watched as they drove off through the snow.

The Bible says that we should give thanks for our blessings. And everyone, I think, had plenty of things to be thankful for. But what is the best way to give thanks? Me, I'd always thought words were best. I always tried to make it a point to do more thanking of God than asking. But how about *showing* Him? Maybe the best way to say thank you to God for our blessings is to use them to bless someone else.

As Christians, we tend to take the easy way out when confronted with the problems of this world. If people are sick or hurting or just down in the dumps, what are the first words out of our mouths? "I'll pray for you."

Which is fine and wonderful. But sometimes the best prayers are the ones we do instead of say.

I didn't know what God had given that man in the Chevy truck, but it didn't matter. What mattered was that he knew he had much because God had given him much, and that meant he had to share the wealth. Not just money. It wasn't the money that boy's parents had appreciated. It was the act.

He did more than give a child a Christmas gift. He gave a family hope. And nothing in life was more valuable.

Pass it on.

# 6

## *Kenny McCallom's Wonderful Life*

There he was, at the end of the aisle moving boxes of cereal around.

Kenny McCallom.

At first I didn't want to speak to him. I felt embarrassed. Not for him, though. For me. Over the years I had made it a sort of unconscious habit to avoid those people with whom I had graduated high school. Most had since gone on to another life in another place. It was easy enough to avoid them. But those who had held true to their roots and remained in town made it a little harder.

If I saw them they might ask me how I was, which was an innocent enough question. But that one innocent question might just lead on down to some other not-so-innocent questions. How I was doing could lead to *what* I was doing, which might lead to the inevitable question of why I was doing it. I know it's complicated. I just didn't want them to ask me what happened, you see. What happened to me, to all of those dreams I had and things I swore I would do. Most of which, of course, never happened at all. I was afraid they would think that instead of striking out into the world, I had struck out in my life. And that bothered me. It bothered me even more that I would care so much about impressing a group of people I hadn't seen in years and never really liked in the first place.

Then again, I thought that maybe Kenny McCallom felt the same way. After all, standing there in front of me stocking boxes of Cheerios was the man who had once stood up in front of his classmates and announced that in ten years he would be spearheading the search for a cure for diabetes.

It was our final assignment for Mrs. Houser's Creative Writing class. An oral essay. The subject was in the spirit of the class's impending graduation from high school to the world beyond: describe what you think each class member will be doing in ten years, and then share what you hope to be doing.

Such assignments from Mrs. Houser were usually met with the expected moans and groans of her students. Not this one. Most of us saw it as a chance to both make ourselves shine and put some of the more haughty members of the class in their place. The idea of sanctioned retribution for four years of perceived inequality was enough to light the fires of impassioned oratory in us all.

The class clown, for instance, eventually signed a contract with a major network for his own sitcom, only to end up penniless and in rehab. The class beauty queen (who also knew she was the class beauty queen) ended up married to a pig farmer. You get the idea.

I made out all right, I suppose. Half the class had me playing baseball somewhere, and the other half had me living
as a hermit in the mountains. I had chosen for myself the
former, but the more I thought about it, the more the latter
made sense.

And then there was Kenny. The boy who sat in the back
row. The class target for all things mean and nasty. The kid
whose clothes were dirty and whose shoes were always a size
or two larger than necessary. Kenny didn't make out so well,
as I remember it. Most of the classmates gave him a mere
passing sentence or two. He was only a waypoint between
the jocks who would end up old and out of shape and the
smart kids who would end up working down at the 7-Eleven.
Most had him carving out a living at either a McDonald's or
a Pizza Hut. Some didn't even mention him at all.

When it was Kenny's turn to stand in front of the class
and perform his own little act of fortune-telling, his version
of the future was much kinder than most of the others. He
let the jocks go on to careers in various professional sports,
all the beauty queens became actresses or models, and the
smart kids went on to become doctors and scientists. All of
which caused a considerable amount of eye rolling from his
classmates.

And then came the time when Kenny McCallom pro-
nounced his own future plans. He did so with an even tone
and a steely gaze. "In ten years," he said, "Kenny McCallom
will be a research scientist leading the search to cure diabetes,
a disease he has struggled with since he was seven years old."

A few of the kids in class smirked. Some smiled. Me, I
think it was the first time I had ever heard him say anything.

And now, all these years later, there he stood at the other

end of the aisle. Turned out that his classmates had, for the
most part, been right. I wondered for a moment how many
other people we had been right about.

And then I wondered if it really mattered. Why did the
expectations of our former selves remain so important years
later? The dreams I had at eighteen were bright and clear,
unmuddied because of a blatant dismissal of reality. We
could dream all we wanted when unencumbered by our
own limitations, but those limitations had a way of making
themselves known as the years followed us. Things often
didn't work out the way we thought they should. That wasn't
reason to convince myself I was a failure, it was reason to
convince myself I was alive. I hadn't been avoiding my classmates all those years. I had been avoiding the me I once was.

"Kenny?" I said.

"Yeah, hang on a second," he said, shuffling around a
few boxes of Lucky Charms. After finishing his task, which
seemed to him to be the most important thing in the world,
he turned to look at me. "Peter Boyd?"

"Yeah. How's it going?" I asked, afraid to know the answer.
After all, the guy was working in the cereal aisle at Super
Mart. How in the world did I *think* he was doing?

"Great, man, just great!" he said with a big smile, sticking
out his hand.

I shook it and smiled. His handshake was strong and sure,
and as I shook it I noticed that Kenny had put on some muscle over the years. He'd been doing something right, at least.

"What have you been up to?" I asked.

Kenny sighed. "Oh, you know, just trying to make a living.
Dude, what happened to your *hair*?"

I laughed and rubbed my bare scalp. "Two kids," I said.

"I hear you, man, I hear you. Got three of my own now."

"Really? That's great. How long have you been married?"

Kenny scratched his chin and thought. "Well, I reckon it'll be ten years come March. Time flies, man."

"You bet it does," I said. "It seems like we graduated just a couple years ago. It's been, what, fifteen?"

"Yeah, I guess so."

There was an awkward pause then as we both stopped to consider the passage of time and how it always seems to speed up when we want it to slow down, and slow down whenever we want it to speed up.

"Did you go to the reunion?" he finally asked.

"Nah. Guess you didn't, either."

"No. I meant to. My wife kinda wanted me to, I guess. She thought it would be nice to put some faces to the names she's been hearing about all these years. But I decided not to."

"Yeah, same here."

There was another awkward pause. It seemed neither of us knew exactly where to go with the conversation and were wondering if it had run its course.

Then he said, "So what happened with baseball, man?"

"Just wasn't in the cards, I guess," I said. "But I can't complain. Everything's worked out fine."

"You remember that essay we had to give to the class for Mrs. Houser?" he asked.

"Actually I was just thinking about that."

"You know I still got that thing at home?"

"Really?" I asked.

"No kiddin'. I don't know why I kept it. I guess it was just pretty much the last thing I did in high school. You remember what I said I'd be doing?"

"No," I lied.

Kenny chuckled a bit, then said, "I said I'd be some big researcher out to cure diabetes. Guess I was a little off on that one."

"Well," I said, "I guess eighteen's a little too early to be planning out the rest of your life."

"I guess so. You never know what's coming down the pike, do you?"

"No, Kenny," I said, thinking about what was coming down my own pike, "you sure don't."

"I mean," he said with another chuckle, "I was about as sharp as a spoon in school. I couldn't even get into college, much less medical school or whatever."

"Well," I said, "if it makes any difference, I was pumping gas a couple months after graduation. I know what it's like."

"There ya go, then. Where are you now?"

"The factory," I said.

"Oh man." He grimaced. "Sorry to hear about that. That place is goin' downhill pretty quick, huh?"

*Exciting Announcement!!!*

"You wouldn't believe it."

"Bet I would, man. Bet I would. Things haven't exactly been all roses and daisies, you know?"

"Oh yeah?" I asked.

"Well, you know, I still got the sugar. It's been pretty hard on me. Doc had to take a toe off me about a year ago."

"Oh. Sorry to hear that," I said.

"Yeah. It's one of those things where nobody really understands it unless they're going through it."

"Trust me," I said. "I know what you mean. My little girl's got sugar."

"No, man, are you serious?"

"Yeah," I said.

"How old is she?" he asked.

"Five. She was diagnosed with type one back in the summer."

"Man, that's awful. I got it when I was seven, you know. How's she holding up?"

"Better than her parents," I said. "She has her rough days, but she's hanging in there. She's a tough little gal."

"I can imagine. But hey, it gets easier to deal with. She'll be okay."

"How's yours?" I asked.

"Better. Not great, you know, but better. My wife, she's got the sugar, too, so we have to keep each other square as far as our diet goes. And, you know, with three kids at home it doesn't really pay for her to work, not with the money a sitter would charge. And she's the kind of gal who wants to stay home with the kids anyway, you know?"

"Yeah, I know," I said, remembering all those conversations I'd had with my wife about the very same thing.

"So it's just me working. We're not getting rich or anything. But what's a guy gonna do? I can't really go anywhere else, but that's okay. I really like it here, and we're doing okay."

"That's good to hear," I said. "How are your kids?"

A twinkle lit up in Kenny's eyes. "Oh man, my kids are great. Claire's almost eight, Dylan's three, and Jamie's almost five. She'll be startin' school next year. I guess we'll be going together then."

"What do you mean?"

"Oh man, yeah, I've gone back to school."

"Really?"

"Yeah. You know, most everybody in that class snickered when I said that I was going to be a doctor or whatever. But I was serious. I might be sittin' here stocking shelves, but that's not what the Lord put me here for, you know?"

"You don't know how well I know," I said.

"So yeah, I'm just seeing where it goes. I took a full load last semester. Lots of science and stuff, just getting my associate's right now. But I averaged a three point six."

"Three point six?" I said, more than a little surprised. "Man, that's pretty good."

"Well, you know, I gotta study. Like I said, I'm about as sharp as a spoon. And man, you should see some of these kids in college now. They think they got it all figured out and under control. Between me and you, they ain't got a clue. But I like it. I think I got it in me. Our doc said that there was a pretty good chance some of the kids will get the sugar, too. It's like a big monster, you know? One I'm still trying to kill."

"You got that right," I said.

"But I don't let it get me down. It drives me, in a way. God might not have given me much as far as stuff goes, but He doesn't need to give people much to make them happy. And I'm happy! I have a wife and kids and a future. I got plenty of time left to do something for the world."

"I hope you do just that," I said, meaning it. "Well, I gotta go, Kenny. The wife needs this bread and milk right now or else catastrophe might set in, and I still have a few more things to pick up before I can get outta all this madness."

"Yep," Kenny said, "you can always tell when it's snowin' with the bread and the milk."

"Good seeing you, Kenny."

"You, too, man. Wow, funny how time seems to slip away from you, huh?"

"Yeah, funny. Or maybe a shame." We stood silent for a few moments, as if both of us were trying to figure out if that slippage of time was comical or shameful. In the end, I settled for both. "But anyhow, you take care of yourself. See ya, Kenny."

"Have a good one."

And we parted. I will admit that I felt a sense of shame and guilt over our little talk. I had always had a tendency to think of myself as a victim, whether of circumstance or God or myself. I was always the injured, the persecuted, the misunderstood. And yet there was Kenny McCallom, a man I had scarcely given thought to in some fifteen years, who knew more about being injured and persecuted and misunderstood than I, thank You Jesus, ever had.

*Why?* That's what I kept asking myself. Why had Kenny been given the life he had? A life of constant struggle not just to get ahead, but to keep from getting behind. A life of toil as a stock clerk at a big-box retail chain. A life of sickness and disease with a wife just as sick and diseased, and one or more children who will likely become sick and diseased themselves.

And there I was, healthy and earning about fifty thousand dollars a year at a job where I mostly just sat around and watched a machine spin liquid polymer into yarn, with a beautiful wife, two beautiful children, a nice house, and money in the bank.

And I was *complaining.* Constantly. Complaining that my job was on the chopping block, that my dreams had never come true, and that life was passing me by.

Passing *me* by? Kenny's life seemed to have already gone over the horizon.

What did he have to look forward to? Maybe fifty more years of daily insulin injections? Of praying every night that he didn't lose any more toes, of hoping that his wife wouldn't get sicker, of hoping his children would be spared from his disease?

It all didn't seem fair to me. But it was nothing new to him. Nothing new at all.

It started at an early age for Kenny. Maybe around Little League, when he was stuck in right field where the ball never went. That way he would never have to try to catch it and never have to throw it.

And then there was school, where he sat in the back row with his dirty clothes and his hand-me-down shoes. That's where his future was cemented, at least in the eyes of the public school system. Somewhere along the line between late elementary school and late junior high, Kenny became known as a number more than anything else. Success to the high school guidance counselors was a 4.0. Kenny's, I guessed, hovered around a 2.5. Success in the eyes of his classmates was a 1200 on the SATs. Kenny never took the SATs. He was by his own admission not the brightest guy in the room, so why bother? But what of his personality, his determination, his heart? What test besides life itself can measure such things?

I paused and looked back at Kenny, who had moved on from the cereal to the granola bars. I felt sorry for him. I wondered about his wife. How did they meet? How did they fall in love? And I thought of his three children and the love they received every day from their father.

And I thought of Kenny returning to school, struggling through his studies to the point where he had an A average, struggling past all of the whys in his life to hold on to a dream of helping give something to make the world just a bit better of a place for everyone. I marveled at him and his faith both in God and in himself. How many people in his position, I wondered, would have both Kenny's faith and Kenny's life? Most, I thought, would have either one or the other. Few would have both.

Yet there he was, pushing on toward his goal, still believing he could make a difference.

And I believed he could. He had already.

No matter how little we have in this life in the way of *things*, we still have much to give in the way of *us*. No matter how bad we have it, someone has it worse, and it's up to us to help them. That was Kenny's purpose on this earth.

That was everyone's purpose on this earth. That's our reason for being here, our *what*. As in, "What shall I do?"

And Kenny was living proof of this fact: as long as we have a what, the hows just don't matter.

# 7

## *The Santa Suit*

Fifty dollars seemed like a lot of money to spend on something I would wear only one night a year, and it seemed like a *whole* lot of money for something I would only wear for a few minutes on that one night. But I didn't have a choice. Some things a father just had to do, no matter how expensive it was or how ridiculous he looked doing it. And I had to do this. *Had* to.

Even if it meant donning a red and white suit, complete with one very itchy beard and more fake hair than Dolly Parton wore.

There was only one Santa suit left, which was a good thing. But it was a large, which was a bad thing. I figured I needed a medium. A large would maybe sag and—Lord, please help me—even fall off while I was making my getaway. That would be disastrous. It would ruin the whole thing.

But I figured I could always just shove a pillow or two

under the suit and hold it in place with the gaudy plastic belt that finished the ensemble. I mean, Santa was a pretty hefty guy, right? Yes, pillows were paramount. And my kids were pretty sharp. They would know something was fishy if they saw Santa and he was skinny.

I put the suit in my cart, satisfied that I was just about to purchase the most important thing I had to get for that Christmas. Or any other, for that matter.

My thoughts returned to the man in the truck and his act of charity. That was no mere act of kindness shown by someone more fortunate to someone less so. It went far beyond that. To Jacob, the act was perhaps some sort of validation. He was at a fragile age for a child. Toddlerhood was gone, but puberty was still a ways off. He was in that in-between time, when confusion reigned and things once believed in were suddenly called into question.

I was about Jacob's age when I discovered the truth about Santa Claus. I had heard murmurings from classmates regarding the eternal lie perpetrated upon the innocent of heart, but I never believed them. Surely, I thought, Santa was real. He had to be. He came to my house every year. Once he had even written his name on a new chalkboard that was propped up by the tree. "Santa was here for Peter and Amy," it said. Proof positive. Though I thought it quite the coincidence that Santa's handwriting so closely resembled my mother's.

Still, the rumors persisted. My faith began to waiver when friends began to tell strange tales of finding their gifts not under the tree on Christmas morning, but shoved into closets and attics weeks before Santa was supposedly to come. I rationalized by thinking they were not good kids anyway.

Santa would never visit them, so their parents had probably felt sorry for them and bought the presents themselves.

But it so happened that one Sunday afternoon in mid-December I was playing with my G.I. Joe action figures in my parents' bedroom, a location that offered the perfect blend of terrain (the tall bed made the use of my new helicopter mandatory) and comfort (the carpet made it easier on my knees). I was locked in pitched battle. The enemy had ambushed a small platoon, leaving the soldiers pinned by the dresser. The number of casualties was mounting, thanks to a nasty little machine gun nest on the top of the bed. I sent in air support to take out the nest, but the fighter was shot down. The pilot managed to eject. After a perilous few minutes of parachuting, he landed at the foot of the bed, where he scrambled for cover. There he planned to hold out until a rescue mission was launched.

When that pilot escaped, he just so happened to get a little too far under the bed. I reached for him and felt something hard. Knowing that Mom and Dad rarely kept anything under the bed, I decided to take a look.

Four packs of baseball cards. One toy machine gun. Legos, Play-Doh, Matchbox cars. My eyes bulged. What was this, some sort of lost pirate treasure? No, that wouldn't work—pirates didn't have machine guns. And birthday presents didn't work, either, since that was still months away.

As I sat there with chin in hand, a disturbing thought formed in the back of my mind and wormed its way to the front. Those presents looked somehow familiar, but how could that be? They were new, unopened. But I knew I had *seen*—

No.

*No!*

I hadn't *seen* them. I had *written* them. In a letter. To Santa.

These were my *Christmas* presents.

And worse, much, much worse, was the fact that my presents were inside several bags from the Super Saver, cheapest store in town.

My first thought was that I must have been bad that year, just like the other kids at school. Santa had gotten hold of my parents and told them he was skipping my house. "I don't give toys to naughty children," he likely said. And as I sat there, mind spinning, I realized he was right. I really didn't deserve anything. Not that year. I'd screwed up too much. There was the time I killed the fish by dumping an entire box of food in the tank. And the nasty little incident where I popped the head off my sister's Barbie doll. And the time when the ice cream truck had come through the neighborhood and I snuck a dollar out of my father's wallet to get some. And on. And on.

On the other hand, I really hadn't done that many more bad things than any other year, and Santa always came through then. Which left only one other possibility. That the kids at school were right. I'd been duped.

There was no Santa Claus.

When I confronted my parents about this, they didn't know what to say. They had never taken time to think of what to tell their children once they were old enough to know the truth. They knew the jig was up. It was confession time. So no, they said, there really wasn't a Santa Claus. There was once, a long time ago, but he was just a good man who gave presents to children. No list, no reindeer, no sliding down the chimney. Oh yeah, and Dad was the one who ate the cookies and drank the milk my sister and I left every year. And the guy whose lap I sat on down at the mall really wasn't Santa, either. He was just some guy whose lap I sat on down at the mall.

More, the letters I sent to Santa every year never got to their destination because no such place existed. There really was a North Pole, but the only things that lived there were polar bears and polar bears couldn't read. Instead, my letters ended up thrown into a big bin labeled *Dead Letters* down at the post office, where they were soon disposed of.

Dead. That's what everyone thought of my letters to Santa.

Mom gave me a kiss on the cheek and a pat on the rear. Dad stared at me and nodded. Both knew the whole thing was rough on me. Both tried to tell me that everything was okay. Just because there wasn't a Santa didn't mean that Christmas wasn't worth celebrating. I would still get my presents, likely most everything I had asked for. Besides, they said, Santa Claus really wasn't what the holiday was all about anyway. It wasn't *Claus*mas, it was *Christ*mas.

They asked me to keep quiet about all of it and not spoil things for my sister. Fine, I said. Whatever.

Ironically, that night was the airing of *Rudolph, the Red-Nosed Reindeer* on television. My sister enjoyed it as much as she'd always had. Me? Not so much.

I grew up that day.

I had reached the point a few months earlier when I decided I didn't want to be a kid anymore. I wanted to be a grown-up and do grown-up things. But at that moment the only thing I wanted was to be a kid again, to forget about all that mess under the bed and the conversation I had with my parents. I felt like Adam and Eve must have when they bit down into that apple. I had Knowledge now, and because of that the world suddenly became something more to figure out than to marvel at. Christmas was only a couple of weeks away, but I wasn't excited. The tree was up and the decorations were hanging on the house, but that just didn't seem to matter anymore. What was the point?

As I pushed my shopping cart through the crowded aisles of Super Mart, I began to ponder what I was going to do when my children made that same discovery. My parents were caught off guard when it happened to me. I didn't want to be caught off guard when it happened to them. Though Josh was in the clear for a while, Sara was five, just two years younger than I was when I found out. And she was already hearing the rumors. At church the previous Sunday a little girl in her Sunday school class told her that Santa wasn't real.

Her parents, I came to find out, had decided that telling their children the truth about Santa was the right thing to do. It helped their little girl to focus on Jesus, they said. The world was too materialistic, and they didn't want their daughter to be that way. Of course, they told me this in the parking lot after church. Next to their brand-new Mercedes. And the father couldn't talk long because he had to get home so he could watch the Redskins on his new plasma television.

Besides, said the father, believing in Santa was bad for other reasons. He couldn't in good conscience allow his daughter to believe in something that wasn't real. That would be wrong. And the whole business seemed to be a bit too occultish for him. Santa was a slippery slope in the spiritual development of his daughter. Why, if they allowed the whole thing to go on unabated, his little girl might even want to start dressing up for Halloween.

God forbid.

Me, I felt differently. I always thought the most important element in a child was a sense of magic, and that quality had to be protected and nurtured. When children are young they see and experience things on a level that adults are simply incapable of. Anything is possible. Everything is cloaked with wonder.

And why not? The world really *is* a magical place, isn't it? Look at a flower or a mountain or the ocean or the stars. Look at a sunset or a butterfly or a platypus. Look at yourself. Magic!

Sara believed in Santa Claus. She had dressed up for Halloween two months earlier. She was a happy child. She laughed often. She lived not in stark reality, but in a world of possibility. Did I think the one had something to do with the other?

Absolutely. And that was something I wanted to always be a part of her.

Which is why I had come up with the idea of buying a Santa costume. Oh yes, I would. And I would be outside of my children's bedroom windows on Christmas Eve, and they would see me and believe all the more. And when I was done I just might drive over to Sara's little Sunday school friend's house, and I just might do the same thing.

A lot of the so-called smart people in this world believe it is their job to explain away everything that happens. Disease and want are not our enemies, mystery is. They believe the three worst words in any language are not "I hate you" or "I am hungry," but "I don't know." That's why every year around Christmas and Easter many of the newspapers and news programs divulge "new research" on the life of Jesus. He was really just a man, they say. A great moral teacher whose message was distorted into a religion. He didn't perform any miracles, He just had a keen medicinal mind. He was more Dr. House than King of kings. He died but did not rise. The Nativity? Unlikely. There is no record of a star above the town of Bethlehem. And a virgin birth? Please. Mary was more likely the victim of rape by a Roman guard.

We would rather have wrong answers than questions. We want facts, not possibilities. We would rather not believe in supernatural things. Not just because those things aren't scientific, but because those things would inevitably lead to God, and we *cannot* believe in God because then we would be held accountable for the things we do in life.

My children believed in Santa. He saw them when they were sleeping and knew when they were awake. They knew he wanted them to be good, but they also knew he would still love them if they weren't. They loved him because he laughed much. He was their favorite person because his delight was to spread joy abundant.

My children also believed in God. They knew He saw them when they were sleeping and knew when they were awake. They knew He, too, wanted them to be good, but they also knew He would forgive them when they weren't. They saw Him as a loving father rather than a distant relative, as someone who laughed much, who was patient and joyful and jolly.

Dare I thought such, but Santa was God 101 for a small child.

It was hard for their tiny minds to wrap themselves around the mystery of the Almighty. It was hard for my bigger brain to do the same. Hard for everyone, sometimes. But Santa we all understood.

Still, I knew that eventually the time would come when my children would realize there really wasn't a Santa Claus. I could buy a costume and stand outside their windows, I could climb onto the roof and ring bells, I could utilize every ounce of my creativity, but sooner or later the game would be over. What would happen to my children then? How would they deal with that loss of innocence? Would they lose that sense of magic and possibility?

Not if I could help it.

The picture of Jacob finding that toy tractor in his parents' car flashed through my mind again. But this time, so did something else. It was the picture of that old man in the truck, sipping his coffee and watching it all. And I had my answer. I knew what I would say.

No, I would reply, there is no Santa Claus. At least not in the way they have been led to believe. Usually the truth hurts, but in this case it is much more wonderful. We're all Santas, you see. We all have magic. The pretend Santa gets to work only one day a year. But we, the real ones, we get to work every day.

We get to spread joy. We get to give gifts. We get to help those who need help and plant smiles where there are frowns.

There is magic in this world, I will say. God is the magician. And we are His hands.

# 8

---❄---

## *Is Anybody There?*

I made a few more stops and crossed the last item off my list, which was laundry detergent. That's all it said. I didn't know what kind of detergent my wife used to wash the family's clothes. Felt a little guilty about that, too. It seemed like something I should have taken the time to find out. But rather than call home and ask, I decided to pick a detergent on my own. I chose Cheer. Not so much because it had something the other detergents did not, but just because I thought it sounded good. *My family could use some cheer,* I thought.

"*Help!* Is anybody over there?"

Shouts, from one aisle over and about two rows back. Elderly and male, by the sound.

"*Would someone please help me?*"

Shouting has definite and strange effects on people. Take the dozen or so who happened to be in my vicinity just then. Just a moment before we were all a mass of busy shoppers in what could be described as one step below a frenzy. One *small* step. There was commotion all around—some people gabbed away on cell phones, others were in conversation with whoever was brave enough to come to Super Mart with them, and some, barely managing to hang on to what little sanity they had left, simply muttered to themselves. We were all consumed by the business of our own little lives, close in proximity but nicely separated in thought from everyone else.

*"I need someone to help me here!"*

But the shouting snapped us into one consciousness. For a brief period, time ceased to exist. Every conversation, every movement, every thought stalled.

What to do? That was the question I supposed was on everyone's mind because it was the question on mine. Shouts mean one of two things—trouble or anger. Both things people tend to avoid being around. So for a moment we all stood frozen, waiting for our fight-or-flight instincts to kick in.

*"Is anybody there?"*

Most flew. But they at least made their exit with a cool ease, an I-was-leaving-anyway-really-I-was departure that belied a sense of cowardice. Others took a more forthright approach and chose to feign temporary deafness. The I-choose-not-to-hear-it-so-it-really-isn't-happening ploy.

Some, however, did not ignore the shouts.

One was a man wearing an EMT jacket. No doubt trained to excel in such situations, he proceeded toward the sound with a sense of confidence. Shouts were a part of his everyday life, a hazard he was equipped to handle and handle well.

Another was a middle-aged woman, short in stature but tall in stride. She gripped her purse close to her side and strode off about four steps behind the EMT. "World's Best Nana" was stenciled on her sweatshirt. A grandmother. Also used to screams and shouts. If the EMT was there to heal, she was there to comfort.

A man in a cowboy hat filed in rank behind her. Big mustache. Bigger boots, which clomped forward with authority and purpose. Whatever was happening, I suddenly felt much better. Who better to have around in the middle of an emergency than a cowboy?

Last but not least, tearing past me with a power that almost knocked me smack into a display of boxer shorts, was a young man in fatigues. His presence made sense. Soldiers don't run from danger, they run to it.

And then there was me, dragging behind the pack. My fight-or-flight instinct was stuck in neutral. What could *I* do? I couldn't keep him alive like the EMT, couldn't comfort him like the grandmother, couldn't keep things cool like the cowboy, and couldn't protect him like the soldier. But the angel on my shoulder was screaming at me to move it, so I did.

*"Is there anybody to help me?"*

Yes.

The five of us converged upon the shouts, along with just about every Super Mart employee in the store. We all stopped and stared, trying our best to process what our eyes were seeing.

Standing in the middle of the aisle, all by his lonesome, was the man behind the noise. Late sixties, dressed in khaki pants, white Oxford shirt, and a blue sweater. One hand held a cane.

The other held a skillet.

"What's wrong, sir?" asked one of the employees, who

must have run the entire length of the store to lend aid. His voice was cracking and his eyes were bulging, as if he was either about to catch his breath or have a heart attack. I thought for a minute that the EMT would have to work on him first.

"How much is this?" the man asked, lifting the skillet up to the employee's face. "It doesn't have a price on it."

Again, silence all around. At first there was confusion on everyone's face. Each person in the group seemed to come to the reality of the situation at their own speed. There was no emergency. No blood. No danger. Just an old man alone in the cookware aisle who couldn't find the price of a skillet.

The adrenaline that had rushed through all of us was beginning to wane. The cowboy was the first to move off, and he did so without a word. He no doubt expected such things to happen when large groups of people converge in one place.

Once the grandmother was convinced that things were fine, she left as well. But not before making the comment that she was glad no one was bleeding. Helpful to the end.

Going, too, was the EMT, though with a great deal of reluctance and what looked like a bit of disappointment. But the soldier stuck around. Just in case.

The store employees stuck around too, though not for long. Some rolled their eyes and tucked away yet another nutball customer story for their lunch break. Some began to laugh. Others, like the poor guy who'd just run the Super Mart marathon to get there, were pretty angry.

"Sir," he said. Nothing followed. He could say no more, though I still couldn't read in his still-bulging eyeballs if he was mad or just out of breath.

"I'll check the price," said another employee, hoping to get the situation over with so she could go back to tending to the rest of the flock of shoppers.

"Thank you," the shouter said.

"Why did you do that?" another employee asked. "You didn't have to scream like that."

"I needed help," said Shouter, shrugging it away. "What was I gonna do, just wander around?"

The young girl who had gone off to find the price returned. The skillet retailed for fifteen dollars and ninety-three cents.

"Thank you, pretty lady," said Shouter.

The employees scattered then. All seemed a little more than agitated, to tell the truth. They didn't need anything like that to happen. Not on that day. Not with the snow and the Christmas crowd.

Me? I smiled. I applauded the shouter on the inside. I couldn't condone his methods, but I couldn't argue with the results. The man needed help, pure and simple. Wasn't shy about asking for it, either. That fact alone gained him my admiration. After all, I'd known plenty of people who needed help but never asked for any.

There was Dr. Benson, for instance. Great guy. One of those doctors who didn't act like a doctor. Not stuffy or overbearing or aloof. Going to see him almost made you feel good about being sick. He lived with his family on a farm at the outskirts of town. I was just entering high school when Dr. Benson developed cancer. He caught it too late and it spread too quickly.

His doctors gave him three months. Three months to get things settled, to prepare himself and his family. Three months to say good-bye. He did say good-bye, I suppose, but he never gave his wife and children the opportunity to do the same. He never told them about his cancer, never told them he was dying. Not until the last few days, after it was too late. In the end, he was alone. And so was his family.

And there was Jack Taylor, who lived three streets over from me. Another great guy. He, too, had a wife and family. And he, too, was successful. So successful, in fact, that he had retired by the age of fifty. Jack and his wife took to the roads for a few years after that. They were always going somewhere to see something. Then the grandchildren came, and Jack decided it was more fun to stay at home. "Family first," he always said. He always said a lot of things, usually ending with a laugh. He had the exact life that I wanted when I turned fifty. I wanted the constant smile and the presence of family and friends. The man had it all, as far as everyone in town was concerned.

Which made his suicide all the more puzzling.

Angela Ward needed help, too. She was sixteen and at a party one night when she decided to take just one hit of methadone. One and done, she promised herself. She kept that promise, too. But then at the next party she had another. And another. Her addiction took hold a few weeks later. She was in trouble, and she knew it. But rather than anger her parents or disappoint her friends, she decided to handle things on her own. No big deal.

But it was a big deal. She overdosed a year later.

There was no doubt in my mind that the shoppers and employees who had answered the shouter's calls for help thought he was a lunatic—or a jerk. All that commotion over a skillet? What a waste of time. How embarrassing. But I didn't see his actions as foolish. I saw them as gutsy. It takes some people a lot of effort to ask for a little help. And to even think of standing in the middle of a crowded Super Mart and scream for it? No way. That's crazy.

Maybe. But maybe it's less crazy than not shouting for help when a disease cuts your life too short. Or when depression grips you to the point where you think you cannot possibly go on. Or when addiction claims you and you keep saying yes when all of your being is shouting no. Silence may sometimes be golden. But it can sometimes be deadly, too.

I couldn't speak for Dr. Benson or Jack Taylor or Angela Ward. I couldn't know the reasons why they never sought the help they needed. I could, however, speak for myself. There were many times when I needed help but kept quiet. Oh, I was good with the little things: "Could you pick this up at the store for me?" "Lift up on that end, will you?" "Could you stop by and give me a hand with the truck?"

But then there were the big things: "I'm feeling pretty down, and I don't know why." "I'm worried about something and I can't stop thinking about it." "I'm scared and I can't shake it." Those things I kept inside. I never really took the time to figure out why. But as I strolled off back into the crowd of busy shoppers, I took a few minutes to do just that. The answer I came up with surprised me.

It was pride. I had always considered myself more humble than proud, and yet there it was. Asking for help meant I needed something that I could not provide for myself. Assistance was required. And there were times when I just couldn't bring myself to let go of my macho manliness and admit that. All this time I was secretly reveling in my own sense of self-sufficiency. I thought I could do anything and get anything and be anything, all on my own. That was a great idea in theory. Not so great in application, though. All the junk a person keeps inside never really goes away. It just sits there, piles up, and starts to smell.

My walking meditation about all of this took me into the book section. My list had been taken care of, and now it was time to do a little shopping for me. I began with the fiction titles and worked my way down. Near the end of an aisle was a section titled "Self-Help." A burgeoning market, I noticed. There were lots of self-help books, all offering advice on everything from how to keep healthy to how to look young to how to be happy.

All different variations of one common theme—you can change your life and make yourself better, and you can do it all on your own. You don't need God. You don't need anyone. All you need is this book and a little determination.

I walked on, stopping to glance at the new calendars for the upcoming year. My eyes wandered from puppies to NASCAR to lighthouses, then settled upon one of the Shenandoah Valley. I picked it up, curious to see if any of the pictures were familiar. The photographs were beautiful, but October's was especially so.

It was an aerial shot taken in autumn. The Blue Ridge Mountains stretched out on one side. The Allegheny Mountains lined the other. The mountains were covered with a carpet of red and orange trees. The valley stretched into the distance between them, a maze of farmland and quiet country roads. It was a wonderful shot, one that made the purchase of the entire calendar well worth the money. I closed it up and tossed it into the shopping cart.

Then I realized something else.

I pulled the calendar back out and flipped to October

again. There was my reason for not always keeping everything to myself. There was my confirmation that we all need a little help sometimes. That we can't all do it alone.

Yes, we were wonderful creations. Made just a little lower than the angels, the Bible said. Capable of many great and wondrous things. But whenever my pride took over and I began to feel as though I never needed anything from anyone, I would remember this: even God needs the help of two mountains to make a valley.

# 9

*One for the Good Guys*

There was a secret to getting out of Super Mart without having to withstand the purgatory of the checkout line, and that was to find a cashier who wasn't stationed in the front of the store. I took a chance and wheeled my shopping cart into the cubbyhole dedicated to all things Christmas, and lo and behold, there was an open register.

I placed my items on the small surface by the scanner as the cashier—Carrie, according to her name tag—slid them one by one over the laser with the efficient rhythm of long experience. Each item inspired a loud beep of electronic recognition.

"Busy today?" I asked.

She looked at me—puzzled or annoyed, I couldn't tell—but with a slight smile. *What do you think, genius? This is a store at Christmas!* the look said.

"Oh yeah," Carrie answered, popping the gum in her

mouth. "We're pretty much busy all day this time of year. And with the snow, it just gets worse. But that's okay. I don't mind."

I nodded and smiled and decided to keep quiet. Carrie put up a good front. Her long brown hair swished from side to side as she scanned the groceries, and each time she moved her left arm the Santa pins on her smock tinkled. And no matter how much she wished she were anywhere on the face of the earth besides sitting behind a cash register that day, the smile never left her face.

Carrie announced the total with a sigh, then quickly recovered with a retail smile. I slid my debit card through the machine and waited for the register to spit out a receipt. Then I scribbled my name and gathered my bags.

"Merry Christmas," I said as I turned to leave.

"Happy holidays."

My smile turned to a wince as I neared the doors. They stuttered open to reveal the promise of sweet freedom ahead, but there I stood, bounty in hand.

If there had been people waiting in line behind me, maybe I would have kept going. I would have simmered a bit, then I would have gone home to my family and eventually put it out of my mind.

But the checkout line was empty, and I had let too many things slide lately. There wasn't much I could do about my life and nothing I could do about my job, but I figured I could get myself a "Merry Christmas." I deserved it.

"Carrie," I said, turning around. "That's your name, right?"

"Yeah," she answered, a little cautiously.

"My wife and I shop here a lot. Groceries, movies, stuff like that. In fact, we're probably some of your best customers."

"Uh-huh."

"And I would guess that, as one of your best customers, you would like to make me happy."

"I'm married," Carrie said, flashing her wedding ring in my face. "Sorry."

"No, Carrie. It's nothing like that, nothing at *all*. I just wanted to ask if you'd be kind enough to exchange my 'Merry Christmas' for one of your own."

"Oh," she said. "No. Sorry. We're not allowed to do that. It's sort of a rule here. We don't want to offend anyone."

"I won't be offended, Carrie," I said. "Promise."

"Sorry," she said. "But have a great day and thanks for shopping at Super Mart."

Thanks for shopping at Super Mart.

"M-e-r-r-y C-h-r-i-s-t-m-a-s," I said to myself through clenched teeth.

I pushed my shopping cart through the electric doors and back into snow. The slush became clogged in my wheels, forcing me to literally drag it to my truck. I was no longer in the same lighthearted mood I had been enjoying earlier. I was mad now. Beaten again. Not by fate or circumstance, but by the happy holidays.

I walked to the other side of my vehicle, opened the door, and then shut it.

No. This fight wasn't over. Not by a long shot. Because in the end I wasn't fighting for me, oh no sir.

I was fighting for sweet baby Jesus.

Back into the Super Mart I stomped, straight up to the old man who was tending the shopping carts.

"I would like to speak to the manager, please," I said.

"What's that?"

*"I would like to speak to the manager, please."* I tried not to shout.

"Wha's this about?"

"Christmas."

"Huh?"

*"Christmas."*

"Oh, Happy holidays to you, too," he answered.

Grrr.

*"I need the manager."*

"Okay, okay, keep your shirt on," he said. Then he walked away mumbling.

He returned a few minutes later with the manager in tow. The mental picture I had formed in my mind of a middle-aged man with thinning hair, a bad mustache, and a sorry attitude proved to be wrong. This lady had grandma written all over her. This was going to be harder than I thought.

"Yes, sir, can I help you?" she asked.

I smiled and said, "I sure hope so. I came in here a bit ago and said 'Merry Christmas' to the cashier. Nice girl and all. But she wouldn't say it back to me. All she would say was 'Happy holidays.'"

She looked at me as if I were a kook. I tried smiling. It didn't work.

"Sir," she began, "it's a store policy—"

"—yes, ma'am," I said. "I got the whole rule thing from the clerk. I just don't understand why that rule got written."

"We just don't want to leave anyone out, sir. We don't want to offend folks of other religions."

"What could people find so offensive about Christmas?" I asked. "The peace on earth, or the goodwill toward men?"

She said nothing.

And then I noticed something. I noticed what was hanging from the chain around her neck. It was tucked into her shirt, but it peeked out from the top when she crossed her arms.

"You're wearing a Jesus fish!" I blurted, pointing to her necklace.

"Excuse me?" she said.

"You're wearing a Jesus fish necklace."

"It's called an *icthus*," she answered. "And yes, I am."

"That means you're a Christian," I answered.

"Of course I am."

"Then...what...I...." I trailed off, my brain in overload. "You're a Christian. You celebrate Christmas."

"Yes," she said.

"Then why can't you say 'Merry Christmas'?"

"Like I said, sir, we don't like to offend anyone."

"*Why is Christmas so offensive?*" I said again, and this time I practically yelled it.

"To be honest, sir, I really don't know. I don't get it, either. But that's just the way it is."

"Look, ma'am," I said, "I know that not everyone celebrates Christmas. That's fine by me. But why let this time of year go to waste? Take a look around. People are struggling. Hurting. But they don't need a deal on ham or half off on a new television, what they need is a little vacation from wherever they are to wherever they think they should be. This time of year is for everyone. It's a time for joy and togetherness and giving. Love and magic and hope. You can't sum that up in 'Happy holidays.' But you sure can in 'Merry Christmas.'"

Nothing. At first, anyway. But after that, a faint twinkle in her eyes. Not of surrender, but of agreement.

"Come on," I said. "You know you want to."

For a moment, I thought I had lost her. But then, just when I was about to thank her for her time and walk away, she leaned in close to me.

"Merry Christmas," she said, almost in a whisper. Then she did her best to hide the smile that was bubbling onto her face. It was a wonderful smile. A beautiful smile.

A Christmas smile.

"Thank you," I said. "And a Merry Christmas to you, too, ma'am."

I turned around and walked toward the doors. As I passed the old man handing out the shopping carts, I patted him on the back and gave him a "Merry Christmas," too.

"Huh?" he said.

I walked out of the store and back to my vehicle. The snow had begun to taper off a bit, and the clouds had begun to thin. Even the sun hinted that it might peek out, giving me hope that if one storm could ebb, then so could another.

I checked on my bread and milk and other things, which were doing quite nicely in the cold backseat. After a few minor adjustments to the radio and the heat, I pulled out of the parking lot and headed for home.

It had been a pretty good trip, all in all. We had our requisite bread and milk to see us through the storm. Josh had a Superman costume for Santa to bring—who, I found out, was alive and well and driving a Chevrolet truck. I saw someone from high school I hadn't seen in years. I learned a lesson from an old man with a skillet. And there were Charlie and Helen, who taught me a thing or two about beauty and love. Add to all of that the fact that I had just struck a blow against the evil of modern culture, and I was having a pretty good day.

Real good, as a matter of fact.

Yep, things were looking up.

A postscript is called for here. The next year, the store initiated the return of baby Jesus to the season. No more assurances of blandly happy holidays for its customers. Out were the generic songs and nonoffensive quasi-salutations. In were the carols and "Merry Christmas." It seems I was not the only one to protest.

# 10

*The Two-Lane Road*

I knew who it was the moment his truck crested the hill about a hundred yards in front of me. Bobby Barnes. Had to be. No one else in town drove a jacked-up red Dodge, and no one around here looked that mean from that far away.

I figured I had about twenty seconds to decide whether to acknowledge him or not. The etiquette was muddy. I had known Bobby since childhood. I knew his wife—I guess that's ex-wife—Carla, and both of their boys. Bobby was a friend. Old Bobby, anyway.

But the guy coming over the hill wasn't Old Bobby anymore. He was New Bobby now, and I didn't care much for version 2.0.

Fifty yards away brought him close enough for me to make a positive identification. I could see his trademark blue baseball cap and Uncle Jesse beard even with the sun bouncing off the snow. Should I wave, just out of courtesy?

I didn't know. Old Bobby would want a wave. Old Bobby would already be flashing his high-beams and swerving in and out of my lane just to get my attention. New Bobby, though? He might swerve over into my lane and not swerve back, hoping that somebody somehow got hit. That was New Bobby.

So maybe I should just do nothing. Just pass him like a stranger. Because that's what we were now. Just two people passing on the road, me going one way and him the other, both on the two-lane and through life.

But that didn't seem right, either. I wanted to believe that Old Bobby was still in there somewhere. That time and circumstance hadn't completely killed him. It might take some life-changing event to bring him back, something like what had changed him into the person he'd become. And maybe it could also be something as small and incidental as a wave on a snowy December day from someone he once knew.

Twenty yards away. Time to make my decision.

*This is so stupid*, I thought. *Just do it or don't.*

No, I corrected myself. This wasn't stupid and it wasn't a simple matter of either doing or not. This wasn't just a wave. This was reaching out to someone who had gotten himself lost. Yet reaching out to someone, even with such a simple gesture, may do more harm than good. Especially when you do not want to be reached. At *all*.

Ten yards.

Reaching out won the mental toss. I threw up my hand and waved, even shook it from side to side a little just in case he didn't see me. Bobby drove past with both hands firmly attached to the steering wheel.

Maybe he didn't see me. Maybe he was just concentrating on navigating through the snow.

Maybe. You never know.

The present consensus around town was that Bobby Barnes was going to hell. Even Bobby agreed. "I'm Bobby Barnes, and I'm going to hell" was how he introduced himself to the strangers who brought their vehicles into his shop for repair. Some didn't really know how to take that. Others thought it was just about the funniest thing they had ever heard. "Well, welcome to the club!" was what a customer once replied. They both had a good laugh over that one.

It wasn't that Bobby was an evil man. Nor did he deny God His existence. He was just a man who had been turned around in life, which happens to a lot of people. Sometimes it's a gradual turn. Other times, a hard one. Bobby's was so hard that the pull made him let go of most everything that mattered to him.

I had met Bobby during a summer Bible school over twenty years earlier. *Summer* and *school* were two words I did not care to put together. Throwing *Bible* in there didn't make things any better. But I went, mostly because Mom wanted me out of the house and around other kids. "It'll be good for you," she said.

She was right. Bible school was okay. Not so much the sitting in church and learning Bible stories part. The playtime part. Hide-and-seek especially. You haven't lived until you've played hide-and-seek with thirty kids.

It was a very democratic process. All kids took a turn being It whether they wanted to or not. There were varying opinions as to the value of hiding rather than seeking. Me, I didn't like hiding. Hiding was boring. It was rare that I could go more than a few minutes without either laughing or getting the jitters, both of which would get me found in short order.

I loved being It. I loved the seeking. It felt better to wander about and look than to be cooped up in the same old place and quiet. And I was good at it, too. I always found everyone except Bobby, a feat that was considered perfection. In most games of hide-and-seek, finding everyone was considered the only way to win. Not for us. Finding everyone but Bobby was good enough. It was universally accepted that Bobby Barnes was the best hider in Bible school, and several of us considered him the best hider in the history of the universe. Nobody ever found him in the four years he was at Bible school—a record that exists to this day, at least around here.

Everyone wanted to know Bobby's secret, but he kept mum for years. "A magician never reveals his tricks," he'd say. But when we were pretty close friends he confessed to me. His secret was that he always hid in the cemetery. A brilliant tactic. No kid in his right mind wants to go in the cemetery.

As good as he was at hiding, though, Bobby was bad at seeking. He would take his required turn being It, count to fifty, and then wander around, doing the absolute minimum before calling, "Olly olly oxen free!" and ending the game. It was a confidence booster for the younger kids who hid in the obvious places. The more experienced players, however, felt cheated. They knew Bobby never tried. All he ever wanted to do was go hide again.

Hiding was "his thing," Bobby would tell me. But not

seeking. Definitely not finding. Even Bobby admitted he couldn't find water if he fell out of a boat.

His parents began accompanying him to church on Sundays. Bible school had a good effect on their boy, and they were curious as to what Jesus could do for them, too. And as it turned out, Jesus could do quite a lot. They were all baptized on the same Sunday a few months later. Bobby's father began teaching a Sunday school class about a year after that, and his mother chaired the visitation committee.

Bobby soon found his niche in the church, too—mission trips. He took his first trip to a Native American reservation out West, which lit the unexpected fires of wanderlust. He was gone for a week every summer after that. Sometimes closer to home. Many times not.

He opened his own repair shop after he graduated from high school. He could fix a vehicle almost as good as he could hide, and maybe better. Transmissions, motors, brakes, anything. If it was broken or squeaky, you took it to Bobby. He was happy then, as happy as I had ever seen him, and it showed. "I'm doin' my thing," he told me once while fixing a busted gauge on my truck. "I love doin' my thing."

One sunny April morning, in limped a dying Toyota Tercel driven by the prettiest little lady Bobby had ever seen. Her name was Carla, and she was late for work. Bobby told her that she had a busted alternator and it would take a while to fix, but he would gladly give her a lift. She gave him her phone number as a thank-you. Everyone thought they made the perfect couple, and they were right. Bobby and Carla's wedding was a thing of beauty.

Bobby wanted to continue his mission work, and Carla was more than willing to tag along. They would close up the shop for a few weeks every summer and strike out into the world to spread the gospel. Africa. Bolivia. Russia. Brazil. Ireland. The two were unstoppable. The only thing that slowed them down was the birth of their twins, Matthew and Mark.

The boys had just turned six when Hurricane Katrina blew through the Gulf Coast in 2005. Carla had family in Mississippi. They managed to get out in time, but their house was destroyed.

Katrina shook Bobby. Like the rest of us, he bore witness to the aftermath every evening on the news and via reports from Carla's family. He decided it was up to him to do his part. God would want that. God would *expect* that.

One Sunday before the sermon, Bobby asked the preacher if he could say a few words.

"I know you've all been watching the television about what's going on down in New Orleans," he said. "They've finally started getting some relief in there, and the government's asking anyone who wants to help to head on down. Carla and I have talked about this, prayed about it, and we've decided to take the family down there for a while. I think God's calling us to do this, and I'd appreciate all the prayers and help you could give. The Lord has shown us what He can do in our lives. I think those people down there need to know what He can do in theirs."

Bake sales and car washes ensued. Special collections were taken. Donations were given by local businesses. A few weeks later, the Barnes family was on its way to the Big Easy, which by then was the Big Disaster.

That was the last I saw of Old Bobby.

They came back three months later. I saw Carla one day

at the bank soon after they had returned. She said the trip was hard on them all, but Bobby especially. "He's so sensitive, you know," she said. "Something happened to him down there. I don't know what. He's not the same as he was. He won't talk about it, either. I've tried. But it'll all come out sooner or later. Bobby can't let stuff simmer inside him for too long before he lets it all out."

She was right.

A few Sundays later the Barnes family was in church again, and once again Bobby asked the preacher if he could share a few things before the sermon began.

"I just need to get something off my chest," he told the congregation. "I'd like to talk about our trip to New Orleans for a minute."

He looked at the floor and shuffled his weight. "I thought it would be a good experience for my family. That it would show us what God was really like, you know? And boy, it sure did. You people wouldn't believe what it was like down there. You can watch all the television you want, but it don't matter. You just have to be there. You just have to see it for yourselves.

"Carla and the kids, they had it pretty good. They stayed in the safe part of the city, you know, tending to people and fixing meals and such. They did a good job. I'm proud of them."

Carla and the boys smiled.

"Me," he continued, "I had the dirty work to do. I thought I'd be going down there to fix things up, you know? But there wasn't much left to fix, really. It was mostly just stuff to clean up and tear down.

"Going into the houses, that was the worst. It was horrible.

One guy found a body that was all bloated and green and had been chewed on by gators and Lord knows what else."

There was a small gasp from someone in the back. Carla sent a pleading look to Bobby from her pew, but he simply shook his head.

"No," he answered her and everyone else. "I gotta tell you what it was like. It's important. That's the truth. That's the way it was. People cryin', walkin' around like they're zombies because their hearts were gone and their minds had just shut down because they couldn't handle it all.

"I saw parents who couldn't find their children. They didn't know if they were on a bus to Houston or somewhere out in Lake Pontchartrain. I talked to kids who had watched their mommies and daddies get swept away by the water and the wind. And I...couldn't handle it. I mean, I just couldn't.

"I'd sit and pray and ask God what I should do and say. But down there in that hell, He didn't talk or do anything. There was nothing. And I would pray and pray, I would *beg* for Him to show me why this all had to happen. But I got nothin'. No words. And I started to feel squeezed, you know? Like God was just squeezing me and squeezing me tighter. And I just couldn't take it anymore."

Bobby paused for a moment, gazing out to the congregation. "I prayed to God that this trip would change me and my family. I can't speak for them, but I can say it sure changed me. I went down there to show those poor people what God could do. I didn't need to do that, though. They'd already seen what God could do."

Carla looked up at her husband. A look of panic flashed across her face.

"We talk a lot in this church about how most of the bad things in this life are because of us or the devil or something. That might be true. We all live in a fallen world, no doubt about that. But Katrina? That wasn't us. *We* didn't do that. That was God. God made that storm, and God killed those people."

Carla's concerned look was now mirrored on every face in the church.

"Me," he said, "I can't sit here anymore and sing about what a friend we have in Jesus. Those people didn't have a friend in Jesus. And I'm sure all those kids would rather have their mommies and daddies back than have a friend in Jesus. Am I wrong?"

He looked at the congregation, then at the preacher. No one answered.

"Am I?"

Carla began to sob.

"I can't worship a God that does stuff like this to people. We have enough to deal with on our own, you know? I still believe in Him, I guess. But I can't worship Him. I can't tell people God loves them, because I don't know if He really does. But I'll tell you what I do know. I'm not coming here anymore. I'm puttin' my Bible away. I can't read it. I've tried a couple of times, but every time I start I just see that body pulled out of that house or those kids cryin' for their parents or those parents cryin' for their kids. I can't speak for Carla or the boys. But I gotta do my thing, and this is it."

With that, Bobby Barnes stepped into the aisle and walked out of church for the last time, leaving his sobbing wife and his two sons alone in their pew.

Some in the congregation began to cry, Bobby's mother

among them. The preacher stood up and walked to the podium to speak. No words came.

Months passed, and Carla hung on as long as she could.

She was sure Bobby would find his way back. "He's so sensitive, you know," she would repeat to everyone who asked. "He'll work it all out. He has to." But by then he was New Bobby, and there appeared to be no going back.

The most immediate changes were visible at the shop. The marquee sign out front was changed from *Life is short, pray hard* to *Oil Change $28.95 State Insp $10.00.* Gone as well was the picture of Jesus knocking on a door that had hung over the cash register. "He can knock all He wants to," Bobby told a customer one day. "Ain't nobody home anymore." He even started opening on Sundays from ten to three. He didn't have anything else to do, he told people, so he might as well do his thing.

Carla took the boys and left soon after that. She knew by then that the family would never be the way they were. She felt horrible about it; part of her felt that God wanted her to stay, that maybe she would be the one to bring Bobby back again. But as much as she tried to convince her husband to come back to church, Bobby tried just as hard to keep her away from it. He would hide the car keys on Sundays so she and the boys wouldn't be able to go. He began drinking and threw her Bible in the trash one night after an argument. In the end, Carla felt as if she had to make a choice between her husband and her God.

Carla married again last year, a nice man who loves her and treats Matthew and Mark like his own. She's happy now, as happy as anyone's ever seen her. But living in a small town like Mattingly means that ex-husbands will often run into ex-wives, and Bobby and Carla are no different. I've seen them in the grocery store and at the gas station, and I can tell that Carla will always love Bobby. Both the old and the new.

Bobby's business trailed off a bit once word got around about what happened. It bounced back, though, once everyone figured out that New Bobby could fix a transmission just as well as Old Bobby could. The eventual destination of his eternal soul became a secondary consideration to how well he could use a socket wrench. People generally have enough to worry about in their own lives. As for what's going on in someone else's, well, that's their business. We all make our own choices in life. We're all just trying to get by.

What bothered me was that before that last mission trip, Bobby was a much better Christian than I could have ever hoped to be. He had more faith, a stronger commitment, and a greater sense of purpose. And still, with all that, Katrina had convinced Bobby to turn his back on his faith. In the end, he just had to do his thing.

I supposed that after all these years, Bobby Barnes was still playing hide-and-seek. Maybe we all were in our own little ways. Sometimes it feels as though God goes hiding, and we all have to take our turn at being It. Bobby's turn came down on the shores of Lake Pontchartrain. He cried out to God in his anguish and doubt, but he didn't get the sort of answers he wanted.

Bobby said God was squeezing him instead of comforting him. I'd always wondered about that. While that might have been true, I didn't think God was trying to hurt him. I thought God was trying to hold him as tightly as He could. Bobby wanted reasons and words of comfort. God knew that the reasons were beyond what Bobby could possibly understand and that the comfort he needed could never come from mere words.

What Bobby needed was God. Just God. So God hung on to His precious, injured child, hung on tight, until Bobby would stop flailing in his despair.

But Bobby couldn't wait that long. Like I said, he was never any good at seeking. Bobby hated being It. So he did what came naturally. When Bobby played hide-and-seek back in Bible school, he hid in the cemetery. Here all these years later, he was hiding among the dead again. Only this time it was the living dead.

But the rules were different now. This time Bobby was having a hide-and-seek with Someone who played much better than a bunch of eight-year-olds. We were too scared to go looking for Bobby in the cemetery. Not only was God not afraid of walking among the dead, He came down here willingly to do just that.

"Where are you?" God said to Adam and Eve after they bit into the apple, thereby starting the first game of hide-and-seek ever. What a strange question for Him to ask. God knew exactly where they were.

The question is, did they know?

Did Adam and Eve know the extent to which their world had just changed? Did they know that with all their new-found knowledge, they could still never undo what they had just done?

"Where are you?"

A question posed to every person who has ever walked upon the world since. It was a question Bobby faced as he hid and God sought.

"Where are you?" God was asking. "Doing your thing, I

see. Are you happy? At peace? Do you finally have all you wanted? No? Then why don't you try My thing instead? It's much better, I promise. Olly olly oxen free!"

I dropped my hand back to the steering wheel and sighed. It was a good try, I thought. And I wasn't going to give up. Bobby might not have been able to put all the pieces of his life back in place, but that was no reason to throw out the whole puzzle. We could all start over. It was one of the great beauties of life.

I hoped that Bobby played by the rules. I hoped that one day he would come home. That he would quit hiding and maybe even see that seeking really is the fun part of living. You never know. You just never know.

Bobby's rear bumper passed mine. My eyes froze when I stole one last look into the rearview mirror. I saw something. It wasn't much, and maybe it was something else entirely, but it was definitely something.

Bobby tapped his brake lights.

*Tap, tap, tap.*

I tapped mine, just to make sure.

He tapped his again.

You just never know. The nice thing about a two-lane road is that it goes both ways.

# 11

## *More Than We Can Bear*

My cell phone rang just as I turned onto the main road leading home.

I remembered hearing a theory once that cell phones were the new cigarettes. You saw people with cell phones glued to their ears the same way you once saw people with cigarettes hanging out of their mouths. Everyone had a cell phone now. It was part of the new, modern age. People could talk to one another no matter where they were or what they were doing.

It was a pity, though, that we rarely had anything worthwhile to say to one another.

I glanced down at the caller ID. It was Sammy at the factory. A chill that had nothing to do with the weather ran over me. Sammy never called unless he had news about one of two things: work or baseball. Since it was December and spring training wouldn't start for another two months, that left only the other option. And if it was about work, he wouldn't bother me on a day off unless it was something major. He knew how stressed out everyone in my work area had been lately, and Sammy knew the value of a snow day. He wouldn't mess that up unless he had to.

I nonetheless decided to let it ring. Whatever he had to say could wait until tomorrow. I was trying to keep my vehicle in the road and protect my precious cargo of bread and milk and stocking stuffers in the back. I couldn't talk on the phone. I had to concentrate.

"Hello?" I said, even before I realized I had picked up the phone and flipped it open.

"Peter, what's up, man?" he said.

"Not much, Sammy. Just heading home from the Super Mart. Had to get some bread and milk for the family."

"Bread and milk. Yeah, I guess I'm gonna have to go and get me some of that if I ever get out of here."

"Better hustle then," I said. "Pickin's were getting a little slim already."

"Yeah. Weather sucks, huh?"

"Yeah." I was wondering when he was going to get to the point. I knew Sammy. The more he beat around the bush, the worse the news was bound to be.

"How many days until spring training?"

"Too many," I answered. "So how's things in the land where hope goes to die?"

He mumbled something, which was another sign that he didn't really want to say what he had to say, which meant he was about to do some serious damage to my day, which meant that whatever was coming was—*Exciting Announcement!!!*— really, really bad.

"I didn't get that, Sammy. What'd you say?"

"I said you picked a good day to take off."

"There's never a bad day to take off. Why?"

"Well, they just sent an e-mail around about the announcement."

Another chill.

"Was it as exciting as they promised?" I asked.

"Well, if 'exciting' means people running around here screaming and cussing, then yeah, it was exciting."

"What's it say?" I said, trying to keep my hopes up. I'd been through this all before. The day I was hired, the plant manager told me I had a job for life. Three months later, I was facing a layoff. Six months after that, the company was sold. Another month after that, I was facing a layoff again. I had managed to slide through each time, but I was beginning to think it was inevitable.

"They're cutting nine out of the area. Half. And they're not going by job performance, either. It's strictly seniority." There was a pause. "You know what that means, don't you?"

Yes. I knew what that meant. That meant I was done. I was third from the bottom in seniority. They were cutting nine. Being third was a long way from being tenth.

"So I guess that's it, huh?" I said. The words were hollow and angry, and I didn't care. The money I was making at the factory was money I couldn't make anywhere else. Getting laid off would mean things I couldn't bring myself to think about.

"Don't worry about it, man. They still have to bargain things with the union, and that'll take some time."

"Yeah," I said, "I'm in real good with the union these days, aren't I?"

That got a chuckle out of him. "Oh yeah," he said, "you're

their favorite person. They've threatened to sue you once, threatened to kick you out *twice*, and all because you can't keep your mouth shut."

"I'm all for the little guy, Sammy," I said. "Sometimes you gotta step on some toes to get someone's attention. I don't think they'll fight too hard to keep me from getting cut out of the area."

"But hey, even if you get cut out, there still might be something for you in another area."

"That's a big if, Sammy."

"I know. But it's something, right?"

"Yeah, it's something," I said between clenched teeth. *Something like a load of—*

"Well, I just thought I'd give you a heads-up. I know your phone will be ringing off the hook. I just wanted to let you know before the rumors start to fly."

"I appreciate it," I lied. "I'll see you tomorrow, Sammy."

"Okay, man. Sorry I ruined your day. You're better off, trust me. This place is goin' down anyway. Just a matter of time. And hey, God won't give you more than you can handle. That's the Bible. You know that, right?"

"Yeah. See ya, Sammy."

"Holla."

And he hung up.

My first reaction was to call home and tell Abby what was going on. But there was no sense in doing that. I could tell her when I got there. Until then, at least she could enjoy her nice, quiet day off with the family. I closed my cell phone and flung it over my shoulder. It landed with a swish in a pile of bags somewhere in the back.

I couldn't go home. Not just yet. For five years I had been

bringing my work home with me, taking out my frustrations and anger on my family, and I didn't want to do that anymore. I had to clear my head. Figure things out.

I took the next right off of Route 340 that led past the scrapyard and out to the road that passed by the high school. Jimmy Buffett was singing about trying to reason with hurricane season, and I turned the radio down a little. I was trying to deal with my own storms, and I needed a little quiet time.

*Everything's going to be okay.* That's what I told myself. Things had been bad before. But all those other times it was just Abby and me. Things take on a greater degree of urgency when you have children. What at one time might have been just a bump in the road suddenly looks like a mountain you'll never see the other side of.

What was that Sammy had said?

"God won't give you more than you can handle."

People said that a lot. I'd said it many times myself. It was in that grouping of expressions that spiritual people use as consolations when there isn't anything else they can say. "God won't give you more than you can bear"—it's right up there with "The Lord works in mysterious ways" and "All you can do is pray." But was it true? Was what Sammy said right? It was the first time I had really cared to think about the validity of that statement.

"God won't give you more than you can handle."

Words spoken in the chaos of the hospital or the quietness of the graveside. Words given in comfort and hope that we *can* pull through, that there *will* be a brighter day, and that we *are* stronger than we think. God would shield us. God would put an end to our hurt before our hurt could put an end to us. We gave Him our hearts and our desires and our faith, and in turn He gave us His prosperity and His blessings and His protection. That's the way it worked. The religious life is one of reciprocation. It was all give and take.

Right?

Maybe. But as I drove I tried to think about one verse of Scripture that backed all those ideas up. Sammy had told me the Bible said God wouldn't give me more than I could handle. Try as I might, though, I couldn't place that verse. I knew there was a verse that said God wouldn't allow me to be *tempted* beyond more than I could bear. But that was a different thing altogether, wasn't it?

I thought about my own situation. I was most likely going to lose my job. My wife taught at a private school and made maybe ten dollars an hour. We had some money in the bank, enough to get us through the next two or three months, but then we'd have nothing left. Ten years of savings would be gone and we would have to start from scratch. I would have to go out and try to find another job in a marketplace where there wasn't much beyond pizza delivery and nursing. I would have to deal with the sense of failure I felt as the provider for my family. I would be a thirty-four-year-old husband and father who had to start all over again. Was that too much for me to handle?

You'd better believe it.

So where would I turn? What would I do?

For starters, I decided then and there I would read the Bible. I did that every day, but now I would read it with a greater sense of purpose. I would seek out the promises of God, and I would hold on to them as if my life depended on it. Because it did.

And I would pray. I did that every day, too, but I wouldn't use the sort of canned Lord-thank-You-for-this and Please-bless-this prayers that I had gotten into the habit of saying. I would pray from necessity rather than memory. I would open my heart and my soul and not just my mouth. I wouldn't just *speak* to God, I would *talk with* Him.

I would have to learn to depend upon Him rather than my paycheck.

In short, I could not see the end result of what I was going through. But I could, right there, see the end result of me.

I would become more than I was.

Life wasn't all about pulling through to face brighter days. Sometimes it was about spending some time in the darkness and being soaked by the rain. Life hunted us with a big net, and sooner or later it would draw all of us in. It didn't matter how good or pious or hardworking we were.

But that was not a sad realization for me. It was a good one. I knew that in the darkest night of my soul God would still be there, shining a candle for me and asking me to follow Him. He knew the way out.

And He would give me more than I could bear only to prove that there was nothing we couldn't bear together.

# 12

### Eugene Turner's Luck

The trip to Super Mart had managed to suck my gas gauge from thirsty to parched, so I decided to stop by the local BP on the way home.

It had only been five years since I left my job pumping gas at the Amoco to go work at the factory. Everyone thought I had made the right choice: my wife, my parents, and even my boss said they didn't blame me for leaving. I could make more money at the factory than I could ever make standing behind a cash register. But as I hit the *Pay Inside* button on the pump and waved to a couple of folks, I suddenly realized how much I missed working there. I missed the informality, the closeness. And the money wasn't altogether awful. It paid the bills. In the end that's all that matters, isn't it?

I made thirty-seven thousand dollars my first year at the factory, twice as much as I'd ever made in one year in my life. The next, I made forty-two thousand. Last year, I made almost fifty. That was pretty good money for someone who barely made it out of high school. I felt like a millionaire. But what did all that buy me in the end? Sure, things would be okay for a while. But what about after that? What would I be left with after a few months of unemployment? A truck I soon wouldn't be able to put gas in, a little insomnia, a little ulcer, and a big problem.

I was deep in thought over all of that when my eyes wandered over to the far end of the parking lot. Parked there with a *For Sale* sign in the window was a Hummer. Not one of the pretend models, either. This was the big daddy. And it was Eugene Turner's.

Nice enough guy, Eugene. A regular in the gas station back when I worked there. He would stop every morning for his coffee and his can of snuff, both of which he would finish off sometime during the day as he piddled around town. Eugene was a genuine handyman, and it said so on the back of his truck. Also stated was the clichéd *No Job Too Big or Small* and his phone number, which were emblazoned onto the truck's side panel with mailbox stickers.

Eugene was married—she was called Missy by the town folk, Sweet Thing by Eugene. He also had two kids ("the runts"), a mortgage, and some credit card bills. He worked hard, loved his life, and could never say no to the Cabela's outdoor catalog he said Satan kept sending him in the mail. In other words, Eugene Turner was me.

Except for one small difference. While I had never been one to play the lottery, Eugene once made biweekly pilgrimages down to the 7-Eleven to beg a smile from the gods of fortune.

It was on a Sunday night three years earlier that Eugene

stood at the cash register with a Lincoln in his hand as the ticket machine whirred and screeched and spit out five sets of numbers for the Powerball. He gave a thank-you, shoved the ticket into his pocket, and forgot about it.

Until the winning numbers were drawn the following Tuesday. Until Eugene walked into his bedroom and grabbed the crumpled sets of numbers off the dresser and flipped his old RCA on to channel six. Until he sat there on the edge of his bed in his oil- and grime-soaked coveralls (courtesy of Mrs. Dishman's broken garbage disposal), slack-jawed and shocked beyond coherency as those little white Ping-Pong balls fell into place and the man in the cheap tuxedo read off all but one of the six numbers Eugene's third pick had garnered him.

Eugene Turner had hit the lottery.

Well, not *the* lottery. But five numbers out of six. And how much did five numbers pay? When the man in the cheap tuxedo answered him ("And said it with a smile," he later said, "right at me!"), he fell off the bed.

The ensuing thud sent Sweet Thing and the runts to investigate. Eugene was back on his feet by the time they reached the bedroom, jumping up and down and hollering like a man possessed. And why not? The man had just won almost half a million dollars.

Eugene called Mrs. Howell, told her he would not be coming over the next day to paint her living room, and offered his apologies. The family decided to celebrate by dining out. And there would be no Hardee's for them on that night. No. The Turners were going to Shoney's.

The Turners spent most of that first month living as large as they could. The old Honda and older truck that sat in their gravel driveway were replaced by a shiny Corvette and the Hummer, which opened the door to buying another house. Eugene figured it would be the epitome of redneck to have a hundred thousand dollars' worth of cars sitting in front of an eighty-thousand-dollar home. And if the Turners were anything now, it was not redneck. So they upgraded to a four-thousand-square-foot colonial in a fancy neighborhood that offered everything from a paved driveway to public water.

It was about the middle of the second month when Eugene realized that a half a million dollars didn't stretch as far in reality as it did in his head. The government had taken its share, of course. That still left him with more than he would have ever gotten by puttering around in other people's crawl-spaces and attics. But Eugene wanted to make sure it stayed that way. He had money now, but he needed to make sure he had money later on, too. Which is when Eugene found his holy grail—real estate.

That's when the real trouble began.

His real estate ventures did fine. Maybe too fine. Eugene bought apartment buildings and houses and land and then turned them into profit. He was Donald Trump with a better haircut and a Skoal can in his pocket. His money began to grow, his assets began to expand, his portfolio began to widen, and his life began to fall apart.

All that extra cash found its way into Missy's self-conscious hands. Eugene always spoke of his wife with the words of a man passionately in love, but they were bracketed around what most saw as the obvious. "She ain't much to look at," he would admit, "but she's all mine and she's all I ever wanted."

Harsh, yes. But sometimes harshness and truth can be synonymous, and this was one of those times. Because the truth was that Missy was just plain ugly.

To say that Missy had a series of "procedures" done at the plastic surgeon's office in the city wouldn't be quite right. "Carvings" would be closer. No one really knows how much it all ended up costing Eugene, but I will tell you this: modern medicine lay down with a fat bank account and the result was darn near a *miracle*. Missy loved the new her. Sure, the pain was excruciating. And she found she couldn't smile or cry or make any sudden movements after it was all over, what with all the lifting and tucking and removing and inserting. But there was no doubt about it—Missy was a new woman.

Missy was under the impression that all of her improvements would add a much-needed spark to the physical side of their marriage, but that wasn't the case. The thing about money is that you work harder to keep it than you ever do earning it. Eugene's constant supervision of his properties left him little time to notice his new wife, much less enjoy her.

By the time Missy had taken the runts and told Eugene she wanted a divorce, there wasn't much money left. The real estate market bottomed out, the bills piled up, and Eugene decided to coax yet another smile from the gods of fortune, this time through the horses and slots.

But there was no smile this time. Eugene went bankrupt seven months later.

In the span of three short years, Eugene Turner's life had been transformed and transformed again. The ordinary man who spent his days in muck and mire suddenly became rich. The world had thrown itself at his feet and begged for mercy. But maybe Eugene should have paid a little more attention to all the pro wrestling he watched. Because all that begging for mercy the world had done was just a setup for a sucker punch once he started gloating.

Eugene moved into a single-wide trailer near the national forest on the outskirts of town. He hung his shingle back up—*Eugene Turner Handyman No Job Too Big or Too Small*—stuck onto a used 1997 Ford truck.

Missy moved in with a sister who lived in Charlottesville and endured almost three months of city life before realizing that all the lifting and tucking in the world wouldn't change who she was inside, which was a simple country girl who was in love with her high school sweetheart. She came back home, tore up the divorce papers, and planted a kiss square on Eugene's jaw.

Ask Eugene how he's doing, and he would say things were fine. Things were better now. Like before he had all the money.

I believed him.

I thought of Eugene while I gazed at the for sale sign hanging from the rearview mirror of his Hummer. I wondered where he was on that dreary December morning. Maybe he'd taken a snow day, too. More likely he was out clearing off driveways or parking lots, making his wage for the day. It was a wage that wouldn't be much, for sure. But that was okay. We need more peace than money to get by in life.

Eugene counted himself lucky. That might seem strange, but it was true. He learned something through all of this, and he figured that if he could do that, then it wasn't all for nothing.

Eugene Turner plunked down all that money on the lottery not because he was greedy, but because he was hungry.

Hungry for a life that was not chained to the same old, but one in which he could remake both himself and his family.

Money seemed to be the surest means to that end. I supposed at some point we all were victims of that lie. That in order to improve ourselves we needed more of something rather than less of most everything. In the end, Eugene discovered that his money cost too much. And that often life became less about enjoying our dreams once we had them, and more about reclaiming what was lost along the way.

# 13

## *Finding Life*

Small grins of sunshine again poked through the dour clouds. What little snow was left in them fell from the sky in larger flakes, a final gasp that a few minutes later slowed to a sputtering flurry and then stopped completely. The snowstorm was over. In a few hours the plows would catch up with nature and most of the roads would be cleared. By the next day, things would likely be back to normal. Such were all storms, I reasoned. They poured and howled and threatened, but they ultimately gave way to calmer skies if we just hung on a little longer.

That's what I was doing. Hanging on. Doing so seemed a courageous act until I realized it wasn't. Courage required choice, and I didn't have an alternative. The ride home meant taking the detour again, which meant time. Time to gather my memories and ponder my day thus far. And also time to process exactly what I was going to tell my wife when I got home.

Abby's faith was strong, much stronger than my own. But financial stability and a debt-free life were her mission, and those two things now seemed jeopardized. The stronger our fears, the more our faith is tested. What would the news do to her?

Maybe I could lessen the blow with a little finesse. Sure, I had to tell Abby the truth. But I could dress it up any way I wanted. I could go the positive route. ("Honey, you know how we've been worrying whether I would have to work on Christmas Day? Well guess what? Looks like I'll be home!") Or there was the walk-by-faith approach I'd thought of right after Sammy's phone call. ("Sure, things look bad. But now we get to see what God can do!")

But a tiny thought had been building in the back of my mind since I left the Super Mart. The sort of thought that sneaks and looms and waits for just the right moment to push everything else out of the way and inflict as much emotional damage as possible. That moment happened when I was considering which option seemed best. In those few seconds, the part of me who was certain everything would work out met the part of me who was most certainly not.

The certain me said that either approach would work, that after the initial shock Abby and I would do what we'd always done—bear our struggles with faith. The uncertain me rebutted by saying that not only were those approaches uninspiring, they were inappropriate. News like losing my job should never be shared with an exclamation point.

I spoke to a lone ray of sunshine poking through the clouds. "Could You at least give me the right words to tell Abby?" I said. "I'd appreciate that. And You'd better hurry, because I'm almost home."

By the time I dropped off Mandy's bread and milk, I knew two things. One was that this was an instance in which God had chosen to remain anonymous. The other was that I would just have to tell my wife the whole unvarnished truth.

I pulled into our driveway, shut off the engine, and sat there. My family was inside relishing their snow day, having fun, enjoying life. The lights from the Christmas tree shone through the living room window. Icicles hung from the porch with a gently sloping grace that seemed both artificial and utterly natural. The front yard was still blanketed in a layer of untrodden snow. It was the perfect scene. And there I was, maybe about to ruin it all.

I gathered the shopping bags, careful to leave the Santa suit and the Superman costume, and headed up the sidewalk. My body weight seemed to double with each step. By the time I reached the porch, the world was on my shoulders.

I put on my most genuine fake smile and walked through the door, setting the shopping bags inside. Abby and the kids were camped in the middle of the living room floor by the ottoman, huddled around what had become Sara and Josh's latest infatuation—their Lite Brite.

"Daddy!" Sara screamed. She jumped and sprinted like a tiny linebacker, smashing her head into my stomach with enough force to double me over if I'd taken my coat off. I wrapped my arms around her blond head and rocked her back and forth until we had exhausted our inertia.

"Hey there, sweets," I said.

Sara looked up to me and smiled. "We're playing Lite Brite," she said. "Wanna play with us, Daddy? We're making a clown. It's fun!"

"Pretty lights!" Josh emphasized through his sippy cup. "Pretty lights, Daddy!"

"Maybe in a bit," I told them. "I gotta talk to Mommy first."

Sara released her grip and rejoined her brother on the floor. She carefully placed a black sheet of paper over the front of the box—"It's hot!" she said—and the two studied the task ahead through the soft glow of the light. In an instant I was struck by the sheer beauty of my children, of their perfect peace with the tiny world they inhabited. It was a father's job to keep his family insulated from all the bad, to preserve as much good for as long as he is able. They wouldn't understand what had happened, but what would my news mean to them? And what would it cost?

My eyes then went to Abby, who sat motionless and waited for me to speak.

*Come on, God. Give me something here. Hello? God?*

"It's going to be okay," she said.

"What's going to be okay?" I asked.

"Your job," she answered, putting a red peg into the Lite Brite. "Roz called. Then Sammy, then Jason, and then Ed. And don't worry, it's going to be okay."

The kids were silent, though not because they were listening. The Lite Brite had captured their attention, and I was thankful it refused to bargain for their release. I walked over to the ottoman and sat beside Abby.

"What did they tell you?" I asked.

"That you might be out of a job because you don't have seniority. Jason, too."

"You realize what that means, right?"

"Yes," Abby answered. "But it doesn't bother me. Does it bother you?"

My wife, God bless her sweet soul, always had a tendency to downplay everything that happened. The more serious something was, the more inconsequential it likely became. I, on the other hand, was normal.

"Yes!" I said.

Josh scolded me with a "Shh!" and then added, "We're *tryin'*, Daddy."

"Sorry, bud," I said. Then softer, to Abby, "Well, let's see. We're getting ready to lose about three-quarters of our income. I'm going to have to find another job that won't pay half of what I'm making now, and I'll have to start over again. Which means I'll be able to retire when I'm, oh, around *seventy-five*."

"Thinking a little ahead of ourselves, are we?" Abby asked.

"Yes. *Yes.* It's called looking at the big picture, sweetheart. You should try it sometime."

"Well," she said, pushing another peg into the black paper and getting an "Ooh!" from Josh, "maybe that's your problem. Maybe the big picture really isn't yours to worry about." She reached out a hand and I lifted her up from the carpet, which got me a peck on the cheek as a thank-you. "I'll go start lunch."

Sara, ever ready to make a mess and call it "helping in the kitchen," took the opportunity to join her mother.

"Pretty lights, Daddy!" Josh said from below me.

I slid off the ottoman and landed beside him, scrunching a small pile of pegs.

"Whatcha doin'?" I asked.

"Pokin' holes," he said. "Whatcha doin', Daddy?"

"I'm keeping an eye on you so you don't decide to have a snack of Lite Brite pegs," I said.

Josh nodded as if grateful to have the supervision. "Thissa neat day," he said.

"I'm glad," I answered.

I watched as he focused on one tiny *G* stamped into the black paper covering the Lite Brite. He placed a small forefinger onto the letter and then stared at the piles of pegs Abby had sorted. It was amazing to watch his tiny mind work, trying to sort and figure and make sense of the insensible. Much like his father.

"I like the Brite Lite," he said, mixing the names.

I nodded. "Me, too."

"Mommy says I can only do it once 'cause the pegs make holes."

"Yeah," I said. "Kinda hard to tell where to put the colors if the letters aren't there anymore."

Josh sipped from his cup and said nothing. I took his silence as an invitation to keep speaking. It was always best to talk things out, even if the nearest person can't comprehend a word of what you're saying.

"I guess I'm making a picture, too. I'm just having trouble seeing what it looks like." I touched the black page he was working on. "Kinda like this piece of paper."

"*G* is for green," Josh said, picking up a peg and pushing it through the paper. The lightbulb inside transformed it from dull to sparkly, and he smiled.

"Good job," I said.

"You try, Daddy," he said, handing me a peg.

I studied it in my hand and said, "There's all this big stuff happening, you know?" I knew he didn't, knew he couldn't, but kept going anyway. "But stuff that makes me ask why. Why gets me into trouble sometimes. Who, what, where, and when? No problem. Those are facts. Why's different."

"Just put the peg where it goes, Daddy. Like this." He punched another green peg through the hole, forming the outline of a pair of clown pants.

"*I'm* being *laid off* at the *factory* in a matter of *weeks*," I said. "See how easy that is? Who, what, where, when. Piece of cake. But why? Totally not cake."

Josh's ears perked. "Can I have cake, Daddy?"

"Not right now, sport. I'm just tryin' to draw my picture."

"Mommy says I can't draw the pitcher, but I can put the pegs in."

I stared at my son.

"What'd you say?"

"Mommy says I can't draw the pitcher, but she says I can put the pegs in. It's like a job."

"Your job is to put the pegs in, not draw the picture?"

"I'm not good enough to draw, Daddy," Josh said, "just good enough to push." He pushed in another peg as if to make his point and said, "Pretty lights!"

Yes. They were pretty. But more than that, they were perfect. I had never considered a Lite Brite to be a teaching tool for anything other than following the most basic directions over and over, but I thought then that was perhaps the greatest lesson I had to learn that day.

Abby was right. The big picture wasn't mine to worry about. All this time I thought my life was something I needed to build. Maybe that was wrong. Maybe instead of creating my life, I needed to *find* it. Not by worrying about the big things, but by noticing the little things.

Yes, my life was a black piece of paper. Its substance was hidden and mysterious, and gloriously so. And the whys of my life were simply the pegs pushed into it to let the light shine through.

# 14

*The Great Backyard Exposition*

Daddy, it's time to go out and play."

My daughter was strategically placed between the sofa and the television so I would have to look at her. Not that I could miss her if she were standing anywhere else. Sara was dressed in enough clothing to survive a week in the Arctic. T-shirt, long-sleeves, sweater, and coat on top, two pairs each of pants and socks on the bottom, matching boots, and toboggan hat. She was three times her normal size.

"Sweetie, you think you have enough clothes on?" I asked.

"Yeff," she mumbled from the small opening that formed above her coat and below her hat.

"You look like a giant blue marshmallow."

She laughed and shrugged. At least, I thought it was a shrug. I couldn't tell. Her tiny shoulder muscles barely made a ripple through all of the layers.

"Where's your brother?"

"Getting dreffed."

"Can I finish my coffee first?"

"No."

If Sara were just a bit older, I might have been honest with her and said I had no intention of going outside. I didn't like the cold, and I didn't like the snow. I would much rather stay inside my nice, warm house, drinking my coffee, and maybe catching a Gary Cooper flick on the old movie channel. I would explain that it wasn't very often that I had a snow day, and that when such opportunities arose, one must use them to their fullest advantage. In short, one must be selfish. And yes, I would say, being selfish was generally not a good thing. But it was sometimes, and this was one of those times. The afternoon was going to be all about me. I thought I'd earned that much considering the news I had gotten from work.

But Sara was not just a bit older. She was a child. Children did not understand such things as the need for rest. My two kids fought sleep the way Rocky fought Apollo Creed. Nor did they have an aversion to snow. Something about the fluffy white rain gave them a thirst that could be quenched only by getting wet and cold.

Sara thought the nice, warm house was too confining. She wanted to be out in the world. She didn't like the taste of coffee. She did not fully appreciate the sublime virtue that was a Gary Cooper movie. And she would never understand the occasional virtue of selfishness.

In short, she wouldn't understand my point of view, which meant I would have to go along with hers. Besides, I had promised the kids earlier that we would go outside when I got back from the store. And though I was sadly ignorant of many of the rules of fatherhood, I knew rule number one: don't let your kids down. Carry out your promises. All of them. Always.

"Well," I said, "I guess you're right. Besides, if you stay in here much longer dressed like that, you're gonna hyperventilate."

"I don't wanna hyverbengalate," she said. "That sounds bad."

"I don't want you to, either, and it is bad," I said. "Let me get my coat and my boots. You go get your brother."

She didn't have to. Just then Josh bounded into the living room, ran into the edge of the entranceway, and fell onto his back. I would have been alarmed if he weren't wearing even more clothes than his sister. He lay there struggling like a turtle on its back, and I stopped laughing long enough to pick him up.

"Leff's go, Daddy!" he said.

"Is that you in there, Josh?" I asked, peering deep into the hood that was draped over his head.

"Yeff," he said through shirt and scarf and coat.

"Okay then, let's head out."

A chorus of yays followed us out the door and onto the porch. The sun was shining brighter, and already the sound of melting snow was tinkling through the downspouts. There was a good eleven inches on the ground, but it wouldn't stay there long. The kids must have realized this on some level, because they were suddenly determined to enjoy their time outside to the fullest.

Both launched themselves from the porch and into the fluff like a pair of synchronized divers. They rolled and flipped and laughed and repeated. Sara made a snow angel, then tried to teach her brother. Unfortunately, he had on so many clothes he couldn't move his arms up and down to form the wings. All he could manage was a bloated *T*, so he simply sat up and began eating a handful of snow. That must have been a good idea, because Sara then did the same. In conjunction with just about every child at some point since the late 1960s, she did her best Linus impression and said, "Needs sugar."

As I stood there watching them, I realized activities for snow seemed instinctual. Snow angels, for one. I didn't remember ever showing Sara how to make a snow angel. I asked Abby later on, and she didn't remember showing her, either. I assumed it was part of our DNA, a tiny bit of code that convinced us that it was both good and right to flop down in some snow and start waving our arms and legs. So, too, were snowballs and the throwing thereof. My children didn't throw dirt or sand. They did throw rocks, but only into the creek and never at anyone else. Snow, however, was somehow different. It wasn't long until I was under assault by dozens of small misshaped snowballs. And some larger ones, too, once Abby joined us.

As the kids began a game of Let's Try to Cover the Front Yard with as Many Footprints as Possible, I decided that it was time to start shoveling some of the snow out of the way. Several of the neighborhood folks had gotten a head start on me, and I didn't want to be the man who was the last to clear his driveway. It was a guy thing.

The sounds of snow blowers revving and slicing through their prey echoed through the streets. I was never one for snow blowers, preferring instead a nice shovel and some good old-fashioned muscle. Sara and Josh waded through

the snow to help but soon lost interest. Shoveling was boring, they said.

Snow had always been one of the wider gulfs between
grown-ups and children. Adults wanted to get rid of it as
soon as possible and so get on with their lives; children
wanted to keep it around for as long as possible and so enjoy
theirs more.

I mentioned snow angels and snowballs and snowmen.
I left out one other traditional have-to-do in the aftermath
of a big snow, and that was sledding. I also left that to my
children. There were no hills near our house, therefore if any
sledding was to be done, I would have to pull the load. After
shoveling our driveway and part of our neighbor's, the pros-
pect of pulling the kids around the yard by a rope did not sit
well.

So Josh said, "Daddy, let's sled!"

"Yeah, let's sled!" Sara concurred, jumping up from
behind the snowman she was building. "I'll go get it."

A few minutes later I was trudging through the snow using
a five-foot piece of rope to pull two children in a lime-green
plastic sled Abby and I had bought from the Super Mart
the winter before. Two kids who weighed a combined sixty
pounds and whose clothing weighed at least that. All told,
though, I did have it pretty easy. Neither of my children was
interested in speed. This was not a race, this was an *exposition*.
And on an *exposition*, speed and fear must yield to patience
and wonder. They wanted to survey the yard, front and back,
and not miss a thing.

So I pulled and watched and listened.

We began at the toolshed in the backyard, where the sled
was kept. Melting snow had caused large icicles to form

along the eaves of the roof, and the children were fascinated by their clarity and shape. The three of us stood for a while, talking about how they were formed and how pretty they were. Josh wanted to hold two of them, one for each hand. I made him promise not to try to eat them, and he obliged. But as I reached up to snap two of them off, Sara protested.

"No, Daddy!"

"What's the matter?" I asked.

"You can't pick them off!" she said.

"Why?" asked Josh.

"Yeah, why?" asked me.

"Because they're *pretty*," Sara said.

"Well...yes. So?"

Sara put her hands on her hips, a signal that she was about to lay down some law. "Daddy," she said, "God put *those* there for us to *look at*." She then pointed to another cluster of icicles along the bottom of the shed. They were smaller and not as thick, but still passable. "He put *those* there for you to *have*."

"Oh," I said. "That okay with you, Josh?"

"Yeff," he said.

I bent down and snapped off two of the smaller icicles. Josh, much to my pleasure, accepted them happily. And Sara, much to my pleasure, was satisfied. Her mission was accomplished. The big, pretty icicles were safe. At least until it got a little warmer. But her way made sense. Use only what you need, and don't disturb the beauty. Ecology 101.

We then moved on to the birdfeeder. Josh was adamant that the birdfeeder be kept fully stocked throughout the winter months, even though the robins and the finches had moved on to warmer places. I never saw any value in it.

About the only birds left in town during winter were crows and blackbirds, and who wanted to feed them?

"Daddy, get some birdseed," Josh said.

"I think there's enough in there to last a day or two," I said.

"It snowed, Daddy. They'll be hungry."

Fine. I walked back into the shed and got a scoop of birdseed. As I screwed the top back on the now-full feeder, Josh scanned the snow for fresh tracks.

"You know that there aren't any robins left," I said.

"Yeff."

"Or finches."

"Yeff."

"Just crows and blackbirds."

"Yeff."

"Do we have to feed the crows and blackbirds, Josh?"

"Yeff."

"Why?"

"Because they're still *birds*, Daddy," he said, pulling down his coat so I could hear him exactly. "Just like the other ones."

Another lesson to file away in my dim mind: blackbirds were as important as robins, and crows were as important as finches. Just as the poor were just as important as the rich, and the common were just as important as the extraordinary. We were all people. The only thing that separated us was our prejudices.

Next was the centerpiece of our children's outdoor life. At some point during every trip outside, no matter the time or the temperature, Sara and Josh could be found on the swing set. To them, swinging and sliding were paramount to any enjoyable day. Being deprived of those two things, whether by fate or parental decree, would inevitably result in some sort of breakdown. Bought on sale two years prior for a little over a hundred dollars, the swing set was bar none their favorite toy. It was creaky and rusted and used, and the slide had been ripped from the side of the swing set by a nasty wind a few months prior. It was a piece of junk, in my opinion.

"How about we get a new swing set in the spring?" I suggested as I pushed one child and then the other.

"No!" shouted Sara.

"No!" echoed Josh.

"We could get a shiny one," I suggested. "A new one. One with an extra swing, maybe. And a slide that's hooked onto it. Maybe even both."

The words trickled out of my lips without my knowing, and I shook my head at them as if trying to blow them away before they could reach my children's ears. *How stupid was that?* I wondered.

But at that moment a new swing set became the most important thing in the world, a symbol of defiance in the face of circumstance. Yes, we would have to cut corners. We would have to save our money for the important things. And what would be more important than something that would allow my children to laugh and jump and play? Even if they didn't know they needed it, I knew I needed it for them.

"Don't you like our swing set?" Sara asked.

"Well, it's a little worn-out, I think. It's rusty."

"I like the rust," said Josh. "It looks like the leaves in the fall."

"And we don't need another swing," said Sara. "There's only *two* of us."

"I like our slide," Josh said. "It's funner now that the wind fixed it."

The subject was settled then. There would be no new swing set. I guessed that sometimes new did not equal better, and many times condition does not equal meaning. Just because something was broken down didn't mean it was worthless, whether it was a swing set or a person. Helen and Charlie had taught me that.

After a quick swing and a couple of trips down the slide, I grudgingly allowed a visit to the sandbox. Grudgingly, because the sandbox was always the Middle East of our home. Strife there was constant, wars frequent, and control the only objective. Yet while the geopolitical nuances of the real Middle East were difficult to state, the problem in our sandbox could be stated in four words and one comma: Sara built, Josh destroyed.

Sara would sit on the edge of the sandbox and proceed to construct whatever her heart and head could conjure. Sometimes her imagination would ignite and she would produce a sand castle. Other times it would sputter a bit and she would only manage a simple pile. But Josh didn't care what she built. He employed no artistic snobbery. Castle or pile, once it reached a certain height, that thing was going to come down. Screams and cries and accusations would follow.

And then there was the issue of the shovels. There were two shovels in the sandbox, a purple one for Sara and a green one for Josh, both of which Sara always seemed to end up with and neither of which she would give up. Which led to more screams and cries and accusations.

Once I drew a boundary line in the sand and said that neither could cross into the other's territory. But like a slightly smaller version of Napoleon, Josh refused to acknowledge the boundary and invaded. Open conflict ensued, which ultimately resulted in the closing of the sandbox for a few days. I briefly entertained the idea of buying another sandbox so each child could have his or her own. But I decided against that, believing then that valuable lessons like respect and generosity and sharing would be left out. The kids had only one sandbox, so they would have to get along.

And then one day, something happened. Sara finally realized that if she were to share her abundance of shovels, Josh would likely become too preoccupied to demolish whatever she made. An unspoken treaty was agreed upon between them. Peace blossomed due to the result of one person sharing her abundance with another. If only nations could learn to do the same.

We didn't stay long at the sandbox. Sand was fine in the summer, they said, but it was winter and there was snow. Sand paled in comparison. Around the corner of the house I pulled. The children, who had yet to stop talking long enough to take a breath, suddenly became shrouded in an almost holy silence. We had stopped at what had become the most mysterious part of the yard.

I first noticed the holes during the previous summer. I was mowing one Saturday morning, and near the oak tree by the side of the house were two carefully dug holes about two inches wide. Near those two was another, and another. Puzzled, I stooped down and peered inside. Nothing. I then grabbed a tree limb and pushed it into one of the holes. The limb, nearly eight inches long, went in all the way. I had no clue as to what could have made such a thing. It was much too small for gophers, but too large for ants. I decided that the prudent thing was to fill them in. The kids found the holes fascinating and had no qualms about helping me plug them with rocks and sand.

The next day, the holes were back. Rocks and sand were gone. Suddenly what the kids had once found fascinating was downright exciting. Questions were posed and hypotheses posited. Sara thought they were fairy holes. Josh was convinced that dragons had taken up residence in our yard. He held a minivigil for a few days, but to no avail. "Those dragons must be *fast*," he said.

We filled in the holes again, and again the next day they were clear. I got a little worried that a snake or two might be hiding in one of them. I placed wet sand around the openings, hoping the critter would leave some prints of some kind. The tracks that appeared the next day weren't from a snake, but they weren't from any other critter that I could identify, either. At the children's behest and against my wife's intuition, I left the holes open.

Fall came, and I felt sure that whatever was in there wasn't in there anymore. Still, the children persisted. At least once a day I would find them either outside peering down into the holes or gazing at them from the window. Now the holes were covered by the snow.

"The holes are gone!" shouted Josh.

"No," I said, "they're just under the snow."

"Maybe we should scoop the snow away," said Sara. "Just in case there are fairies inside. They might want to get out."

Josh brought up the possibility of dragons then, and if there *were* dragons in there, he would much rather they *stay* in there.

"I could just dig the whole area up," I offered. "Then we'd know if there was anything under there or not."

But my motion was defeated by two votes. Something *might* be in there. That was all that mattered. If I dug up the holes, then either they would find out what that something was, or they would find out there wasn't anything in there at all. Neither option appealed to them. Knowing *exactly* might spoil the fun.

I agreed with their philosophy and even encouraged it. The holes were my children's first sip of the mysterious, and I wanted them to drink deeply. Life is made more beautiful by the unknown. Somehow knowing that we couldn't ever know it all was comforting.

The kids bid the holes farewell with solemn awe and we moved on to the creek that ran down the side of our property. The water there flowed straight out of the mountains for most of the year, only occasionally taking a break during the summer months when heat was abundant and rain scarce. It was, of course, another preferred spot for my children, who loved any kind of water so long as it wasn't in a bathtub. Sara loved to collect the rocks worn smooth by the water flow, and Josh loved the frogs and minnows that hopped and swam and eluded his grasp.

During July and August, the creek was off-limits. Those were the hottest parts of the year, and as the creek provided the only source of water around, the snakes would arrive to look for a drink and a quick meal. Copperheads and rattlesnakes were few, but still common enough to keep the kids away.

The snakes were gone by September, though, and Sara and Josh would resume their treks along the water's edge. Autumn also allowed them to indulge in their favorite activity at the creek. The oak tree would begin dropping acorns, and the kids would take turns dropping them one at a time into the water by the culvert at the road. They would then follow the acorn all the way along the yard to where our property ended. They did this nearly every day, until the evening became too cold and dark.

The acorns were gone now, too, either buried beneath the snow or tucked away by the squirrels. But the snowfall had knocked quite a few branches from the oak. I watched as Sara and Josh tossed tiny twigs into the water, then alternately ran and walked according to the current. It struck me that such a simple act could produce such a strong reaction. Though I could not see their vessels, I could deduce whether there was trouble or clear sailing simply by observing the children's body language. Both would tense when their branches became momentarily marooned on a rock or a clump of dead grass. Both would relax when their branches worked free. And both gave screams of victory when finally their branches sailed on past the neighbor's fence and into the unknown.

And I realized the heart of their activity. This was not a mere game to them. This act carried some larger meaning. They were being taught a valuable lesson, a small one at the time but one that would become more valuable as the years passed. If a tiny twig in a raging creek could overcome any obstacle to reach its destination, then so could a tiny person in a raging world.

Thus ended our exposition. I pulled the kids over to the shoveled sidewalk, where they disembarked and joined me on the porch. We all slumped down into rocking chairs. After two and a half hours of pulling and listening, I needed a break. It came when my wife sat down with us. The smell of fresh bread and a smear of flour on her shirt let us know what she had been doing all that time. After a quick check of Sara's glucose, she fetched the three of us hot chocolate and went inside to watch the dough rise for her rolls.

The kids and I rocked in silence for a while, each of us lost in his or her own reflections. I realized that I had been granted a wonderful gift, which was the opportunity to see the world through the eyes of children. It was a gift I could unwrap and enjoy every day, if I so desired. But that was the problem. Sometimes that gift simply sat on the shelf, lost in the hectic days or the weary nights. There were plenty of days when I didn't take those opportunities to know my kids. Yes, I played with them. I tucked them into bed. I read them stories. But rarely did those moments come when I was able to peer into their hearts and know who they truly were.

My children were extraordinarily alive. Sometimes that seemed to be more of a curse than a blessing. I would scold them occasionally for being too loud or rambunctious or... mobile. My kids seemed to be in a constant state of flux.

They attacked life. I was constantly in retreat of it. They drank deeply from its springs. I would often take a mere sip and then go sit down for a while. To them, the world was a marvelous place of exceeding wonder and delight. I sometimes felt the same, but that was usually only on Saturdays, or when the Yanks and the Sox were on television.

I was angry with them at times. What parent isn't? But I realized then that it really wasn't anger I was feeling. It was jealousy.

Jesus said that the kingdom of heaven belonged to those like children. I could see why. The world did not pollute them. They didn't know the meaning of doubt. They didn't know greed or hate, only love and joy in abundance. And because of all those things, my children enjoyed a closeness with God I did not. I could hear it in their prayers. I could see it in their lives. I realized then that maybe I'd been doing the parenting thing wrong. I had always tried to turn my kids into me. Maybe I should have been trying to turn me into my kids.

"It's a good day," Josh said, breaking the silence. It was another one of his favorite sayings. This one was spot-on, too.

"It truly is," I answered him.

"Daddy?" asked Sara through her hot chocolate mustache.

"Yeah, honey?"

"What's a bad day?"

I had to think about that. What *was* a bad day?

"A bad day is when people don't realize what God has given them," I said.

And we rocked.

# 15

## *Michael Pannill's Triumph*

My reverie was interrupted by Josh's hot chocolate spilling onto my lap. I jerked my leg away in reflex and turned to him, intending to remind him to watch what he was doing. I changed my mind when I saw that the spill was more the result of shivering than clumsiness.

I glanced over to check Sara, who had been conspicuously quiet for a while herself. Our backyard foray had ensconced what hair was showing under her toboggan cap in a thin layer of ice. A low hum was being emitted through her chattering teeth and her lips had taken on the bluish hue of her coat. Both of my children seemed to remember from the previous winter that playing in the snow was fun, but they actually had to play in it again to remember that it was also cold.

I gathered them up and took them inside, where Abby shepherded them to the fireplace to dry out. Yawns and grumpiness ensued, and all parties agreed it was time for a nap. With children in bed and wife still baking, I decided to go and sit outside a while longer.

Snowstorms have a way of clearing things, whether the air or the mind. They swoop in and put a halt to everything and in their wake leave a stillness in our surroundings that is sadly lacking most of the time. As much as I had always tried to avoid winter by thinking of spring, I did relish that brief period of time just after the last snowflake had fallen and just before the everyday bustle of life resumed. The quietness of a December snow was one of the true pleasures of life, and one I was not going to miss despite my aversion to the cold.

So I sat and rocked, enjoying the silence and knowing it wouldn't last long. The sun was too bright and the melting already begun. Many of the neighborhood children had been outside for a while, and there were a few adults milling about. Those who had not yet appeared would soon creep out to clean off vehicles and driveways. Whatever level of enjoyment to be had would correspond to whatever duties needed to be fulfilled. If the only objective was fun, plenty could be found. But it was hard to enjoy the snow if you were holding a shovel instead of a sled.

A group of juvenile thrill-seekers walked by my house about twenty minutes later. Four boys aged about nine, dragging their sleds behind them. The Baptist church on the other side of the neighborhood was their likeliest destination. There was a steep hill there in the back of the parking lot that had taken many of the neighborhood children on rides through the years, some down the hill and some to the hospital. It was always the place to go when the snowfall exceeded four inches or so.

I noticed that the one in front had both the oldest sled and the rapt attention of the other three. The leader, no doubt. The one with all the sledding experience. He was regaling his friends with tales of the hill. It was steep, he said, *real* steep, and there was no stopping once you started down. And you had to watch for the rocks, too. Some of them stuck out of the ground a couple of inches, and you wouldn't be able to see them with the snow. But you would sure *feel* them, especially if you hit one of them wrong and went tumbling. He told of the boy the previous year who had been thrown by one. He went head over heels down the hill and smacked himself against a neighbor's woodpile. Got a nice shiner for his trouble, too. But just hang on and pay attention, he said, or you're gonna get hurt. Bad.

He stopped cold and turned around to say those last few words, just to add to the drama. His narrative had the desired effect on the other three. They hung on his every word, using his descriptions to concoct a mental picture of the adventure ahead. The paces of the other boys quickened in anticipation.

Well, the paces of two-thirds of the other boys, anyway.

One boy did not seem to be sharing in all the enthusiasm. He walked at the back of the group. Head down, almost in prayer, he seemed pulled not by the thrills that lay ahead, but by the collective will of his friends. His steps did start coming faster a few moments later, though not by much, and only so he would not be seen as a straggler.

"C'mon, Mikey," the leader urged. "We gotta hurry before all the good spots are taken."

"I'm comin'," Mikey said, defensiveness dripping from his words. "The snow's not goin' anywhere."

It was typical male nonchalance that masked an underlying dread. Even from the rocking chair, I could tell something was bothering Mikey. Maybe he was cajoled into going by his friends. Maybe he just wasn't into sledding. Maybe he was a warm-weather guy like me.

Then again, maybe it was all the stuff he was carrying. While the other boys had equipped themselves with the bare necessities—coats, gloves, sleds—Mikey looked as though he were about to enter combat. Kneepads were tightly secured to his thick ski pants, as were elbow pads over his coat sleeves. A bike helmet was strapped atop his head. And he kept fumbling with something in his right hand. When he stuck it into his mouth, I knew Mikey was wearing a mouthpiece.

*Is this kid going sledding or three rounds with Chuck Liddell?* I asked myself, shaking my head.

Mikey plowed on, walking forward and yet glancing backward, toward what I assumed was his house. He flinched as a crow cawed in the woods across the street and then rocked backward as he looked back down at his feet. I couldn't believe it. The boy was a walking cliché. Mikey had jumped at his own shadow. Then, perhaps realizing there was safety in numbers, he lumbered on and caught up with his friends.

A few minutes more produced another group of sledders. Then another. The hill was going to be crowded. Once upon a time I fancied myself quite the sledder. As a kid I never bothered with the hill at the Baptist church, though. It was too far from my house, for one thing. And for another, that hill was purely kid's stuff.

Weaver's Hill was my old stomping grounds, just three houses down and one street up from my boyhood home.

Now *that* was a hill. You needed more than just mere gravity to conquer that behemoth, you needed skill and courage.
You needed to know where you were and where you were
going. An absence of those things was a death sentence. You
just might end up sliding right out into the middle of Wayne
Avenue.

It had been years since I had last grabbed a sled and tack-
led a hill, Weaver's or otherwise. The closest I ever got now
was dragging the kids around the yard in one. Sara and Josh
were still too young to go sledding at the church. I was probably too old to do the same. But that didn't mean I couldn't
go down there and watch.

I stuck my head in the door to check on the family.
Abby was still kneading dough and the kids were still fast
asleep. I figured I had a good two hours before I was needed
again. I told my wife that I was going for a walk around the
neighborhood, just to clear my head of the day's events. She
mentioned an ad in the paper for help at the college in Stanley, and that maybe I should drive up there and put in an
application. I said I would think about it while I was gone.


The sounds of screaming children greeted me as I rounded
the back of the church. It was the sort of screaming that was
half terror, half joy, and all fun—the kind that only children can seem to vocalize. Twenty or so of them were either
zooming down various parts of the hill or trudging back up
it. Most were under the watchful eye of Mom or Dad or both,
who clustered together at the top and gossiped. It was an
almost Rockwellian scene—the snow, the sun, the church,
the kids, the laughter. It reminded me of how blessed I was

to live in a small town, where such vistas were still common but never taken for granted.

A high-pitched "Here I go!" caught my attention. Over to my right, a boy had backed up a good ten feet or so from the top of the hill. Sled positioned perfectly at the edge, he took off in a full sprint and leaped onto his sled. He shot off out of sight, leaving nothing but a trail of whoops and displaced snow in his wake. It was the leader of the pack of boys who had first passed my house a while earlier. I could tell why he was the boss, too. The kid was fearless and confident, even at such a young age. He returned to the top a few minutes later, giving and receiving high fives from his admirers. Some of whom were parents.

It was then that I noticed Mikey. Helmet and kneepads Mikey. Mouthpiece Mikey. He was still managing to be both of the group and apart from it. He whooped it up like the rest of his friends and gave the leader his own high five. But I noticed that even though the rest of the boys were already covered with snow, Mikey was dry. They were cold. He was comfortable.

"All right, Mikey," the leader said. "You're up."

"Naw," he managed. "I gotta wait for the snow to get packed down some more. It's faster that way."

"You've been saying that for ten minutes," another of the boys said. "Get goin' already. You're missin' out."

"I'm not missin' out," Mikey retorted. "Y'all go a couple more times. I don't wanna mess around with that soft stuff. It's boring."

The leader put his sled down and walked over to Mikey, away from the other boys. His words echoed my own thoughts. "Mikey. You scared?"

Whether you are a boy or a man, that is the one question you do not want asked. The male of the human species can be accused of being almost anything—soft or cruel, caring or indifferent, peaceable or hateful—and still manage to retain something of his manhood. But if he is accused of being a coward, there is no hope left for him.

Mikey bristled. "I'm not scared," he said.

"Then go, okay? Sheesh, Mikey, you act like it's some big deal. It's just *sledding*. It's fun. You'll see."

"All right," Mikey said. "I'm goin'. But I don't like it when the snow's soft."

The boy who was afraid of crows and his own shadow, who looked backward to the safety of his home while his friends looked ahead to the fun awaiting them, was out of options.

But then salvation came from the small crowd of parents.

"Mikey?" a voice called out.

One look at the lady sitting among the small group of parents and you knew who her child was. Her chair was one of those portable, expensive ones with the backrest and a cup holder. She held a large bag. Sticking out of the top was an inhaler, a box of Band-Aids, and a package of Ace bandages. She hung the bag on the chair as she called him, and I could hear the shaking of a thousand kinds of pills. Mikey's mom was ready for anything. She probably had a haz-mat suit in there, too.

"Yeah, Mom?" called Mikey.

"Come here, sweetie."

"Come here, *sweetie*," one of the other boys mocked.

"Yeah, come here, *pootie pie*," said another.

"Shut up," Mikey told them both. When you're a boy,

there's nothing you want more than to be a man. And there's nothing like your mother calling you to her with a "sweetie" on the end to remind you that you're not quite there yet.

I quietly shadowed Mikey as he made his way over.

"Yeah, Mom?" he asked.

"Mikey, did you remember to bring your mouthpiece?" she asked.

"Yes, ma'am," Mikey said, patting his coat pocket.

"It won't do you any good if it's in your coat pocket."

"Mom," he protested, "I haven't even gone *down* yet."

"Well, don't you let your friends talk you into going down that hill if you don't want to. I don't know how you managed to talk me into this. It's *dangerous*, Michael."

"I'll be okay. I want to go, I really do."

"Is your helmet on tight?" his mother asked, tightening it anyway.

"Yes, ma'am."

"Make sure you keep it on. When I got here, it was sitting on your sled."

"I wasn't sledding, Mom," Mikey said. "What am I gonna do, slip on the snow and crack my head open?"

It was the wrong thing to say, and Mikey knew it. He looked down and kicked a clump of snow.

"Young man, don't you take that tone with me," she scolded.

"Sorry, Mom. But none of the other boys have to wear helmets. Even the little kids don't have them."

"Well, they are not *my* kids," his mother said, using that age-old argument stopper. "Now you be careful. And watch your asthma. If it acts up, let me know. I have your inhaler in my bag."

"Yes, ma'am."

"Are you feeling okay?"

"Yes, ma'am."

"Make sure you keep your scarf on. The flu's going around."

"Yes, ma'am." Then, "Mom, you don't have to be here if you don't want to. I'll be okay. You can go home. I know you're cold, and I can just walk back with the guys."

It was a valiant if unfruitful attempt. Mikey was at that age when mothers began to be thought of as necessary evils. Necessary because she was still Mom. But also evil, because even though he needed her, he didn't necessarily need her *around*. Especially when he was sledding. With his friends. Who were boys.

"Don't be ridiculous, dear. I'm not cold at all." Her teeth were chattering and her hands were jammed into her pockets and her posture was frozen solid. But she was not cold. "I'm actually quite comfortable," she said then.

Mikey tried once more. "You sure you don't want to go?"

"I'll tell you what," she bargained. "I'll go if you go."

Mikey thought about that. I could tell he was torn. Torn between his mother and his friends, between the hill and his fears.

"No," he said. "I want to stay."

"Suit yourself then," she managed, trying not to show her disappointment and not doing a very good job of it. "Go have fun with your friends."

"Okay, Mom."

"And don't forget your mouthpiece."

"Yes, ma'am."

Mikey rejoined his friends, who began to give him as hard

a time about going down the hill as his mother had about staying away from it.

So he tried to buy himself some more time. He said he wasn't ready yet. That the snow was still too soft. Go one more time, he said to his friends. It'll be good and slick then. Then he could *fly*.

His friends obliged. After all, they were more concerned with having their own fun than making sure everyone had equal participation. The leader, of course, went first and with his customary flair. The rest followed. By the time they all made the climb back up, Mikey was out of excuses, and he knew it.

So did his mother.

"Mikey?" she called.

"Yeah, Mom?"

"Come here, please."

His mother, I saw, suddenly became much more necessary to Mikey than evil. He didn't just trudge over to her like the last time, he practically sprinted.

"Yeah, Mom?" he asked again.

"Mikey, listen to me. I don't think you should go down that hill. It's too dangerous. I know you're scared, sweetie, and that's okay. It really is. If you don't want to go down, you don't have to. I can take you home right now. I'll fix you some hot chocolate and we can watch some movies. It'll be fun. But," she said, probably to assuage whatever guilt she was feeling, "if you want to play, go ahead."

There. Her cards were on the table. I didn't know what kind of a hand Mikey was holding, but I knew it would be hard for him to beat a royal flush of parental guilt. He looked over his shoulder to his three friends, who waited impatiently for him to take his turn.

"Mikey," the leader said, "let's go, man. We ain't got all day."

So this was it. Mikey had a choice to make. Go home and be safe with Mom, or face his fears head-on and become a man. It was an easy decision.

"Mom?" he said, turning to her. "I'm cold. Let's go."

"Oh, you poor thing," his mother smiled. "Come on. I parked in the lot."

"I'll be right there," Mikey said. "I just have to say bye to the guys."

"Sure, honey." She began to gather her chair and medicine suitcase before her son had time to change his mind.

Mikey walked back to his friends. He knew that in order for him to extricate himself from the situation with a little dignity, he would have to deliver some Oscar-worthy lies. And boy, did he.

"I gotta go," he said.

"What?" It was the leader. Mikey was smart enough to direct the statement to him. If the other boys still harbored doubts about his story, they would be more likely to follow along if the leader was convinced. "Oh man. You haven't even gone down yet."

"I know. It stinks. But Mom's cold and she says I gotta go home with her."

"But you came here with us," one of the other boys said. "Why can't she just go home and you can leave with us?"

Uh-oh. Mikey didn't see that one coming.

"Well, my dad's coming home soon, and I have to get my chores done." It was quick thinking, and it was brilliant. All of the boys knew about chores and the need to have them done before their fathers got home.

"Okay," the leader said. "Well, we're sticking around here for a while. Maybe you can come back with us tomorrow."

"Yeah," he said. "Sure thing."

Mikey left them and started toward the parking lot. His mother was already waiting in her minivan, the kind equipped with enough safety features to repel anything this side of an asteroid.

"Come on, dear," she called, trying to coax Mikey along. Victory was within her grasp. She had done her job as a parent—she had kept her child safe. To her, that was all that mattered. It was good that her son was afraid. Fear kept him from danger. From . . . risk. That's what going down that hill was to her—a risk. And it was the sort of risk that many risks were—unnecessary.

But I noticed that Mikey seemed to be holding a different view of things. He was caught between the fears his mother had helped to instill in him, that need to be *safe*, and his desire to break free of them. He knew that if he went down that hill and his mother was right, he may not live to see another day. But he also knew that if he didn't go down, if he did live to see another day, then so would all of his fears.

Mikey stopped.

His mother, still smiling, waved him over to her. "Come on, honey," she said. "It's cold. We don't want you to get sick."

Mikey shook his head.

"Mikey," she said again, "please don't play games. Let's go home."

Again—no.

"Michael Lee Pannill, you get in this van right *now*!" It was loud. It was forceful. Mikey's mom was not playing around anymore. She was losing control of herself, of her son, of the whole situation.

Mikey picked up his sled and ran toward the hill. His friends, transfixed, watched in shock as he flopped down on the sled belly-first and disappeared over the edge.

"*Mikey!*" his mother screamed. "Oh Jesus, help me, help my boy!" She flung the van door open and jumped out, tangling herself in the seat belt she had forgotten to unbuckle. She jerked and pulled and twisted herself free, then sprinted toward the boys. "*Mikey! Mikey!*"

His friends stood frozen, mouths agape. I realized then why. They had all gone down *sitting* on their sleds. Even the leader. But Mikey had gone down *headfirst*. No one did that. It was too bold. Too . . . *risky*.

I stepped toward them, reached into my pocket for my cell phone, dialed 911, and kept my thumb hovering just above the *Send* key. Someone was going to need medical attention very soon. Maybe Mikey. Probably his mother.

"*Aaahhh!*" Mikey screamed. I didn't know if that was the sound of fear or joy. Then he screamed, "*Mommy!*" and I knew. Fear.

Then things got a little worse. Halfway down Mikey hit one of those rocks the leader had warned him about. The sled bucked about four inches into the air. When it came down, Mikey wasn't on it. He tumbled the rest of the way down the hill, then came to a stop when he fell into a bunch of freshly made snow angels.

"Oh Jesus please let my boy be okay!" his mother cried. She launched herself down the hill after him, and to the utter amazement of both the boys and me, she made it all the way down to the bottom without falling herself.

Mikey was still there, sprawled out in the snow.

Laughing.

His mother reached the bottom and nearly pounced on top of him. She checked him over with the skill of an emergency room doctor. Fear turning to rage, she grabbed his arm, jerked him to his feet, and started pulling him and his sled—which, she said, he would "never, *ever* get on again!"—back up the hill.

"That was so awesome!" It was the leader, and it was the ultimate compliment.

"Did you see how fast he went?" said one boy.

"I thought he was just scared," said another. "But I guess he was tellin' the truth all along. He just wanted us to pack the snow down for him."

Mikey's mother was still in shock when they crested the hill. Things had been going so well, but she had failed. It was her job to watch over him. The world was a bad place, eager to devour someone so young and frail and innocent.

But if she was wearing a look of defeat, her son was wearing one of triumph. There Mikey was, being dragged by the arm to the van and sure punishment, and he was laughing. He had done it. He had faced down a fear. It was one of many, to be sure, but it was one and it was the first and maybe the rest wouldn't be so hard now.

He had learned one of life's most valuable lessons: the fear of a thing is usually much more frightening than the thing itself. He learned that playing it safe wasn't always necessarily the best thing. Sometimes you had to cast your bread upon the waters. Sometimes you had to risk it. You had to get bumped and bruised. Sometimes you had to fall. But that was okay, because Mikey found out the angels would catch him when he fell.

He knew all of that then. It was written on his face and imprinted in his heart. He might have gone down that hill as Mikey the little boy, screaming in terror for his mommy, but he came back up it as Michael Lee Pannill, young man.

As the two neared Mikey's group of friends, they tried to rush him with compliments. Mikey's mother would have none of that, though. She whisked him away and into the parking lot.

"You didn't even have your *mouthpiece* in, Michael," she scolded. "I *told* you to make sure you put it in before you did something stupid like that. You could have lost your teeth playing that stunt."

"I'm glad I didn't put it in," Michael managed to say as they walked toward me. "If I had, I wouldn't have been able to laugh."

As they passed me, I quietly extended my hand. Michael bumped my fist with his. I winked. He smiled.

Good thing his mother didn't see.

# 16

## *Eleanor's Story*

Traffic had been practically nonexistent in that part of the neighborhood since I had begun my walk. What little there was had been concentrated down at the church, nearer the main road. All of which made the sound of the diesel engine coming from behind seem all the more loud and out of place. I stepped closer to the side of the street and turned to see what was coming.

Around the corner came the familiar sight of a UPS truck. It zigged and zagged along the slick road, desperately trying to make progress up the slight but steady incline that led to the houses near the edge of the woods. The driver zoomed past while I was still facing him, sending a spray of dirty mist that engulfed me, then pulled over to a house just up ahead.

The normal urgency and economy of movement that is associated with your average UPS driver seemed to be absent

from this one. There was no sudden shot out of the side door
with package in hand. There was no Olympic-worthy speed
walk up the driveway to the front door, no quick ring of the
bell, and no sprint back to head off toward the next delivery.
This driver was instead resigned to his fate. He lumbered. He
labored. He *strolled*. Up the driveway with package in hand,
he rang the bell twice for good measure.

And then waited.

The sight almost stopped me cold. I had never seen a UPS
driver wait at the door of someone's house. It seemed so…
unnatural. These were, after all, people whose daily routine
consisted of constant motion. I then thought that perhaps
the package he was carrying required the signature of the
recipient. Yes. Had to be it.

But it wasn't.

The front door opened before he could glance away from
it. Out stepped an elegant older woman whose smile seemed
as natural as the curls in her hair. She greeted the driver
and took her package. Without even a glance at the box, she
placed it inside the door and turned her attention back to
him. Strange, I thought, that someone would receive a box
and not bother to at least take a look at it. The driver did
not ask for a signature. Instead, he appeared to be hanging
around just for the conversation. The delivery took so long
that by the time he had said his good-byes and made it back
to the truck, stopping for a quick smoke break, I was walking
past.

"How ya doin'?" I asked.

"Good," he said. He eyed my muddy coat and muddier
face. "What the world happened to you?"

"Truck got me," I said, and nothing more.

"Everybody's in a hurry these days," he answered, shaking his head and taking a long drag from his cigarette.

I nodded and said, "Rough day to be out delivering packages," through a cloud of secondhand smoke.

"You got that right. No snow days for us, especially at this time of the year."

"I bet," I answered, suddenly very thankful that I was not a UPS driver. "I guess somebody's gotta play Santa, right?"

"That's me, jolly Saint Brent," he laughed. He paused, then waved his Marlboro Light toward the ranch house he had just visited. "That lady there? I'm Santa to her all year long. I'm by here two, maybe three times a week. *Every* week."

I whistled. "Wow. Sounds like someone needs a hobby."

"She's got one," he said. "She buys stuff."

"Well, I guess I can think of worse ways to spend your time."

"Maybe, maybe not." There was a bit of mystery in his words, a hint that there was more to what he said and he wouldn't mind sharing it with a little prodding on my part.

"Well, I guess there's a limit to what we really need, huh?"

"Yeah, I think so, too," he said. "But this lady, I guess she needs everything I bring her."

"All of it?" I asked. "I imagine you can't even walk through that house, then."

He smiled as he finished his cigarette and tossed it into the road. "Know her?" he asked.

"Nope, can't say that I do." I checked the black metal mailbox by the driveway for a name, but there was none. As a matter of fact, there really wasn't much of anything to the house. No decorations, no flower beds, no chairs on the front porch. A person wouldn't even know that anyone lived there at all if it weren't for the curtains in the windows. One of which, in the living room, moved a bit as I scanned the house.

"Didn't think so," he said, checking his watch. The visit and the smoke break were over, I assumed. Time to get back to work. I was just about to offer a good-bye and a Merry Christmas when he continued: "Her name's Eleanor," he said. "Nice lady. Little reclusive, though. I guess some people are just like that."

"They are," I answered, not bothering to add that I was one of them. "But she's got all that stuff you bring her to keep herself occupied, right?"

"Yeah, that's what I figured."

"The two of you must be pretty familiar with each other by now. I've never seen a UPS driver stop and chat with someone they're delivering a package to."

"Well," he said, "when I started off, I'd just drop the box and ring the bell, you know, like I do everywhere. Then one day the door opens up before I could hit the button, and there she was. 'Thank you, son,' she says. Couple days later, same thing. After that, she just starts talking to me. I guess I expect it so much now that I build in a few extra minutes for it whenever this is one of my stops."

I looked at the house again, and again the living room curtains shifted a bit.

"What's she talk about?" I asked. "I mean, if you don't mind me asking."

"Oh, I don't know," he said. "Normal stuff, I guess, weather and all that. Then I give her the package and she says stuff like 'That so-and-so is so sweet' or 'I've missed talking to this person or that.' "

"Who? Family or something?"

"Nope. They're the people she talks to on the phone when she orders her stuff."

"You're kidding me," I said. "You mean she orders so much stuff that she knows the operators by name?"

"Oh yeah," he said. "Most of 'em anyway."

"What a greedy old lady," I said, shaking my head at the curtains that were moving again. "But I guess we all sometimes think we can buy our happiness, huh?"

"Nah, man," he said with a laugh, "you don't get it. Take a look around. All these houses bunched together like a glorified apartment complex. Fences everywhere. All these people, but even on a day like this no one's at home. Everybody's working, doing their own thing, got their own lives and their own problems. A lady like Eleanor, she doesn't have anybody. She don't order stuff because she thinks those things will make her happy. She orders stuff to talk to the operators. To have a little company."

I opened my mouth and said nothing. I couldn't. I had never heard of anyone doing such a thing. "So," I said eventually, "she's got all the stuff in there that she'll never use just so she can talk to someone?"

"Nope," he said as he climbed back into his truck. "She returns it all. Like I said, she just wants the company." He turned the key in the ignition and the truck came to life. "I figure I can take a few minutes out of my day to talk to a lady like that."

"Yeah, I figure," I said.

"Well, I gotta go. Nice talkin' to ya. Merry Christmas."

"Merry Christmas," I answered.

He pulled off then and left me there alone. Well, almost alone. The living room curtains moved once more.

I stood there and studied the mailbox again. No name, just a number. The driver said her name was Eleanor, though he hadn't bothered with a last name and I hadn't bothered to ask.

*Why didn't I bother to ask?* I wondered.

I looked up and down the street. It was one of the main roads that ran through the neighborhood, a mile or so long from the church to my own street up at the end. Twenty, maybe thirty houses lined each side, most of which were families of at least three. I did the quick math with my head and a few fingers. There were about two hundred people around there, more or less. Probably more.

I realized, too, that I passed by Eleanor's house just about every day. Not only did I not know who lived there, I honestly couldn't recall ever noticing the house at all. How was it possible to miss such a thing? But I supposed that I was always preoccupied with where I was going or just in a hurry to get back. There's a lot you can miss by letting your mind wander out just ahead of everything else.

The living room curtains moved again, and I was sure that Eleanor was trying to get an eyeful. She was undoubtedly wondering what the strange man in the driveway was up to. I could picture her, nervous and shaky, waiting for me to make my move so she could pick up the Pottery Barn catalog and call for help.

What a horrible way to live. I made a mental note to mention her in my prayers when I went to bed. Maybe Abby could put her on the prayer list at church.

People like Eleanor always made me count my blessings. Sometimes you didn't realize what you had until you saw someone who had a lot less. I shook my head and thanked the Lord for giving me people to love and love me back.

"Thank You, Jesus," I said, walking toward home and believing that was the end of it.

There are people who think God doesn't really speak anymore, that prayer is just a message sent via divine mailman who delivers them to God, who then ponders over them and performs His will. I disagree with that notion. I think He speaks often. Not in that grandfatherly voice you hear in the movies, but in more of a whisper to your heart. It's a notion you know didn't come from you, a feeling that just wasn't there before. That's why I can say this and with a great degree of certainty: at three o'clock in the afternoon of my snow day, on Crescent View Drive in the town of Mattingly in the Commonwealth of Virginia in the United States of America in the western hemisphere of Planet Earth, God spoke to me.

"What are you thanking Me for?" the voice said. "For giving you a family? Friends? Well then, you're welcome. Glad to do it. But what about that lady down the road you just blew off? Don't you think she could use a little blessing, too? Oh but that's right, you have your own problems. Job stuff. Wow, that's too bad. I could have used you back there. You think I do all the blessing in the world Myself? Hey, ever think that sometimes I do My blessing through other people? But you just shake your head and say, 'Poor lady.' How Christian of you. Maybe if she's really lucky, you'll remember to say that prayer for her tonight right before you doze off. Maybe you'll make a passing mention of her in church. That'd be great.

"Let me remind you of something. You are a soldier. You are *My* soldier. One of many. And we're all at war. Don't you remember that? Your job is to fight the enemy, not to ignore it. Your job is to heal. It's to piece together. The loneliness that Eleanor is feeling? One of your enemies. And what are you doing? 'I'll pray,' you say. But you know what? You're using that as an excuse to do nothing.

"I made the world such that no one can survive it alone. Some try. Some even think it can be done. But it can't. Love one another: I didn't just say that one time a couple thousand years ago. I say that every day. *Love* is an action word. It means doing something. So do something.

"I didn't build the human heart whole. I left pieces out. I kept the biggest for Myself and then I gave the other pieces to your wife, to your children, to your family and your friends. The rest are scattered about among others, many of whom you don't even know yet. Without those pieces you can still function, you can still live your life and even think you're doing something constructive. But the fact remains that without all of those pieces, you are not what you should be. Not even close. Some people know all of this and spend their lives trying to make sure those pieces are found. Their hearts are whole. Other people don't know. They don't bother trying to find those pieces, and they wonder why they feel so empty inside.

"Your job is to find those pieces, starting with the one I have, and to help others to find their own. Eleanor, she doesn't seem to have too many of the pieces, does she? So why don't you go back there and help her look?

"And just a little reminder—it's not all about you. I know what's going on in your life. I know what I'm doing. Don't worry about it. Quit focusing on your bruises instead of the gaping wounds in others. And Merry Christmas."

It was the first time I had ever heard God speak to me that way. Sort of snarky and sarcastic and nothing at all like Morgan Freeman in *Bruce Almighty*. But I figured God gave us His truth in the way we could best understand it at the moment, and at that moment I thought I needed God to speak to me that way. I needed a kick instead of a nudge. And the end result was just what He wanted. I stopped and turned around.

God was right, of course. I had spent the whole day sporting my what-about-me attitude, pausing briefly here and there to satisfy my curiosity and try to get my mind off things. But my problems were always there, just in the back of my mind, just beyond whatever thought I happened to be thinking.

I had always felt that there were three things you must do in order to make any day a good one: laugh at least twice, tell someone you love them, and do some good. I'd done the first two. But aside from getting Mandy her bread and milk, I'd not done the third. Why? Because I was too wrapped up in myself. Because I had forgotten that I was a soldier in a war not of body, but of spirit. One waged against the effects this world can have upon the hearts of those who live in it.

There were plenty of things in life that we just couldn't fix. But that didn't mean we couldn't necessarily make them better.

I strolled up the driveway and rang the bell. There was silence. The curtains moved again. And the door opened.

# 17

---※---

## *Rules for the Road*

I said my good-byes to Eleanor with the promise that I would visit again. My snow day was wearing on, and if I wasn't careful I wouldn't make it to the college in time to apply for the job they were advertising. If that was what I decided to do. Change was something that came to every life, but that didn't necessarily mean I would welcome it.

Rather than giving in to my emotions regarding the subject, I decided to use a little logic. As I double-timed it up the road toward home, I began a mental list of the pros and cons of working at a college. I was about halfway down the list of cons *(Number four: colleges are usually the abodes of very strange people who harbor some very strange ideas)* when I again heard the sound of an engine.

Around the corner of the next block came a 1969 Mustang. The driver never halted at the stop sign, never even paused, and I wasn't sure if that was because he was unwilling or unable. The fact that the back end of the car was fishtailing convinced me it was probably the latter with much of the former thrown in. The car was too powerful for the slick road and the tires were too worn to grab the slush. I was sure he wasn't going to stop until his irresistible force met the nearest immovable object, which in this case was the house on the opposite corner. For a split second I thought a tragedy was forming before my eyes, but at the last moment the car righted itself.

The close call would have probably been enough to get most drivers to ease off the gas a bit. Not this one. As soon as the grill was realigned with the middle of the street, the car took off again.

"Slow down, Chris!" I yelled as he sped past.

"What's up, dude?" he answered, hanging halfway out of the driver's side window and waving. I started to yell again, but it would have been pointless. Chris was already around the next corner.

Chris Davies lived a few streets over with his parents and a younger sister. Nice family. And Chris was a nice guy, though a little reckless sometimes. And in the three weeks since he'd turned sixteen, he'd been reckless a lot more often.

Our culture generally marked off the passage from child to adult by the signposts we pass. Getting a driver's license was among the first. Chris passed his driving test without incident, though he did admit to throwing up that morning from nervousness. The picture on his license betrayed his true feelings about the accomplishment—all teeth, little face.

Of course, the test itself was the easy part. Learning to drive is not something one grasps at once. It takes both time and a measure of humility to learn the rules of the road, and those were two things Chris had in short supply at the moment thanks to his girlfriend, Heather. Who, by the way, was also a cheerleader. When you're sixteen, time doesn't matter. And when you're sixteen and dating a cheerleader, humility tends to get tossed out the window.

"There's only one rule to driving," he told me one night.

"And what's that?" I asked.

"Don't get caught." Then he laughed, held up his hand, and said, "Come on, dude, give me one!"

I didn't.

As my father said when I was Chris's age, the only real cure for stupid is self-administered. Chris would have to find out on his own that the rules for driving were not constricting laws, but Reasonable Directions.

That was what Chris's father called them. I had watched him teach Chris to drive, the two of them traveling up and down the road with varying degrees of success. Chris always had a look of sheer joy plastered on his face. His father used to look as though he were sharing a ride with the angel of death.

His dad decided to implement what he calls Reasonable Directions. Principles that, if heeded, would keep his son out of both trouble and the hospital. He drilled Chris in them. He hung them on the refrigerator in the kitchen and tacked them onto the wall beside Chris's bed. Chris once rattled off the Reasonable Directions to me, giving them as much thought as he was giving his life.

It occurred to me in that moment that Chris had yet to discover that learning to drive a car was a lot like learning to drive a life. Both revolved around laws whose mechanics may be difficult to understand but whose results were easily seen. Operating a vehicle was nothing but an exercise in physics. The laws of force, mass, and acceleration all applied. And living was nothing but an exercise in the spiritual in which other laws such as the Ten Commandments, the Golden Rule, and the Sermon on the Mount were called into play. Following the Reasonable Directions would help keep you safe, whether on the road or in your life.

So maybe it was appropriate that the first signpost of adulthood would involve getting a driver's license. There was much wisdom to be found in that act. And as with all wisdom, you just had to dig a little to get it.

I still remembered Chris's list of Reasonable Directions. The first one was *Be safe*. There is a lot of danger in life. Some of it sits and waits for us to stumble upon it, and some of it is out there trying to find us.

Another one was *Keep it slow*. We're always in a hurry, aren't we? Always trying to get somewhere to do something so we can go to another somewhere to do something else. Better to slow down. We miss too much by rushing along.

What about *Pay attention*? Good advice for the drivers around here, since there are a lot of country roads with potholes and ditches. Don't watch where you're going and you'll find yourself in the woods. Keep your mind on things that don't really matter in life, and you'll likely find yourself in the woods, too.

*Check your mirrors* is also important. Since we tend to associate with those we share common traits and values with, the friends we have and the company we keep are mirrors of ourselves. So, too, are our children. They come into this world as blank slates, and for the first years parents are the ones who hold the chalk. What they become is often our own self-portrait, just miniaturized.

*Heed road signs* to be aware of specific road rules—Stop, Yield, Merge—that if disobeyed will land you in front of a judge. But there are plenty in life, too. Warning us, helping us, keeping us safe. Heed them and all may not be well, but it would likely be better. A good thing to keep in mind, since we'll all have to stand in front of the Judge one day.

*Never drive while impaired* was most certainly a good idea. When driving, that means no alcohol or drugs. When living, that means no hate and fear. Because those things impair us, too.

I was thinking about all this when the Mustang made its way back up the hill, fishtailing again. From a block away I saw that Chris must have come to his senses a bit since I had seen him last. He was probably going only thirty now instead of forty. I stepped into the middle of the road and waved my arms for him to stop.

"Need a ride, dude?" he asked after he rolled down the passenger's side window.

"No, Chris, that's okay. I value my life."

"Huh?" he said, not hearing me over his blaring radio.

"*No thanks!*" I yelled.

He fiddled with the knob and the music stopped. "Gotcha. Hey, what were you yelling at me when I passed you last time?"

"I was telling you to slow down."

"Ah, come on. I got this," he said through an I'm-ignorant-of-my-ignorance smile.

"Chris, you have to stop acting like an idiot around here. You gotta be safe. You gotta slow down. Pay attention. Don't you remember the Reasonable Directions? Act like you got some sense."

"I remember," he said. "But when I get home after going out, I don't wanna say, 'Gee, that was nice.' I wanna say, 'Man, what a ride!'"

I shook my head and sighed. Chris Davies. Sixteen years old, and he thought he was the indestructible, all-knowing, all-powerful master of his life.

"Have a good walk, dude," he said, laughing. "I'll be sittin' by the fire all nice and toasty by the time you get halfway home."

He threw the gearshift into first. "Don't you remember the last Reasonable Direction?" He waved with a laugh and left in a cloud of exhaust.

I thought for a moment and then smiled. His father had wanted to end things on a high note, because following Reasonable Directions isn't designed to make things less fun, but to make us more happy. The last item on his father's list was evidently Chris's favorite.

*Enjoy the ride.*

As I kept walking, I couldn't help but think he had a point. Life isn't just about playing it safe all the time. Sometimes it is worth taking a risk. In life, maybe we all need to take a curve too quick sometimes, just to keep things interesting.

Of all the things we long for in life, it was comfort we craved the most. Comfort was what had taken me to Super Mart for bread and milk. It was what Helen had gone to the park those many years ago to find. Kenny was going back to school to earn his family comfort, and Eugene was trying to buy it with that lottery ticket.

And that was now what I was losing. I had followed the

rules. All of them. I had kept my life slow and paid attention. I had checked my mirrors and watched for signs. But despite it all my comfort was being taken away. It was a theory we were all taught early in this world, but one that still baffled us each time it was proven true: sometimes you could do everything right and still have things turn out wrong.

Some people would say that was life, and I supposed it was. But it was also God, I thought. Maybe God wasn't as concerned about our comfort as we were. Maybe things like trust and faith meant more. Which was why He would allow us a little discomfort sometimes. We would hurt a little, yes. But we would learn more. We would learn that when the smooth road we're driving upon ends at a cliff, He'll be there to catch us. Knowing that seemed important to me. It was the difference between covering my face in fear and spreading my arms in anticipation.

*Enjoy the ride.* Yes. That was my favorite rule, too. And one much easier to obey if I realized that pain had its purpose in my life. That the deeper it bored into my heart, the more room it made for joy later on.

# 18

## Beary

I walked through the front door expecting to hear the sweet silence of two napping children, but I was instead greeted by a living room in shambles and the television loud enough to rival a Metallica concert. Sara and Josh sat on the floor and feigned ignorance at the mess of toys and coloring books surrounding them. Not their fault, they promised. They had no idea how all of it had gotten there.

The dining room, too, had been relegated to pigpen status since I'd left. Abby was busy washing clothes and had forgotten the cardinal rule of raising two small children—never turn your back for more than two minutes. Dolls, trucks, clothes, Legos, marbles, and dominoes were scattered over the dining room table. It looked as if Santa had arrived early and tripped on his way to the tree.

I sighed and crept through the minefield of pointy action figures and Barbie supplies to the bedroom, where I searched the closet for my favorite sweatshirt. Comfort was key when it came to a day off, and if there was anything I needed, it was comfort.

I explored through the shelves and hangers. Nothing. The next pass met with the same result. I even went through Abby's side, knowing she had a propensity for lounging around the house in my shirts. Still nothing.

A tinge of panic began to build until I saw a frayed gray sleeve poking out from the bottom of a pile of clothes on the top shelf. Yes! I reached up and pulled, expecting to free it without upsetting the delicate balance. And it almost worked. Halfway out, my sweatshirt decided to bring its friends along for the ride. As if I'd pulled a keystone, the entire contents of the shelf tumbled down and onto my head. The force of the cotton and denim, along with a few softballs I had forgotten about, buried me on the floor.

"Help!" I called from beneath the pile. "Avalanche!"

No answer.

"Anybody?"

Through the clothes I heard the muffled patter of tiny feet coming down the hallway, then an even more muffled, "Daddy?"

"That you, Josh?"

"Whatcha doin', Daddy?"

"I'm trying to get dressed."

"Try harder, Daddy."

"Thanks, buddy."

I rose up through the clothing like a monster out of the mire and did my best scary voice. Josh laughed and launched himself toward me, knocking me back into the pile, and then made a hasty exit before I could ask him to help straighten everything up.

It didn't take long to decide the top shelf was in fact the Bermuda Triangle of our closet. Things were put there and then lost for no apparent reason. I found a sweater Abby had given me back when she was just a girlfriend. I found another an aunt had bought me that I never managed to summon the courage to wear. There were T-shirts I hadn't seen Abby wear in years and blue jeans that would never again fit me. It was a shocking and embarrassing moment—half of our closet was filled with things we never wore.

I piled the clothes on the floor and walked into Josh's room for comparison. His closet was smaller and crammed with so many clothes and stuffed animals that it was almost cartoonish. Sara's was just as bad, filled with all sorts of things from clothes that no longer fit to games she no longer played to stuffed animals that wouldn't even be accepted by Buzz and Woody.

It was ridiculous, our excess. How could anyone possibly be happy with so much stuff?

I gathered my family in the living room and made an executive decision. We had too many things, I announced. We should feel awful. There were plenty of people around town who hardly had anything to wear, and there we were with so many clothes that we could never wear them all. And the kids had so many toys that they had forgotten about half of them. Something had to be done, and we were going to do it. Today.

"What toys?" asked Sara.

"Your stuffed animals," I said.

"I like my stuffed animals!" protested Josh.

"You can keep a few of them, but just a few. You don't need them *all*, do you? You have your own private zoo in your closet."

He said nothing and bowed his head. It was an attempt either to entreat God to his defense or hide the tears puddling in his eyes. I wasn't sure which it was, but I was sure I didn't want to push the issue.

"What are we gonna do with them?" Sara asked.

"I'll take them to the firehouse," I told her. "They'll give the clothes to the poor people and the stuffed animals to the children whose houses catch fire."

"Jesus loves the poor people," said Josh, head still bowed.

"He does," I answered. "And He wants us to help them as much as we can."

The motion was seconded by Abby and carried by Josh. Sara abstained, choosing instead to sit on the sofa and stare out the window. I tried and failed to read the look on her face.

I distributed one trash bag each to the kids, and Abby and I took two for ourselves. "Put in there whatever clothes or stuffed animals you don't use," I said. "I'll take a look at them when you're done."

Abby and I carried our bags to the closet, where we imposed an eight-month standard on all clothing. Anything not worn since the previous winter would be tossed into the bag and given away. It was a good theory in principle, but one that proved difficult in application. There was, for instance, a hat I really didn't want to part with. Technically speaking, I hadn't worn it in the past eight months. But as it had been caught in the Bermuda Triangle on the top shelf, that wasn't my fault. If I would have known where it was, I surely would have worn it. And if I surely would have worn it, I couldn't give it away. The logic was impeccable. There were also shirts that had likewise been forgotten but satisfied my tastes just fine, and three pairs of jeans that still fit.

Abby had similar problems. She found a skirt that would fit just fine once she lost those nagging couple of pounds, a sweater she could not part with because a good memory had been woven into it, and so on.

We agreed the eight-month rule was not a good one to apply to this particular situation. Better to just get rid of the things that were too worn or too ugly and spare ourselves the mental exhaustion of having to keep coming up with reasons why we needed to keep something.

Our trash bags full, we ventured into Josh's room to check on his progress. Since he was only three years of age, I was prepared to find anything. Anything except actual clothes and stuffed animals inside his trash bag.

"Look, Daddy!" he said. "I can't fill it *all* the way, 'cause I'm small."

It was a good point, and I said so. I tousled his hair and gave him a pat on the rump for a job well done.

Sara was not in her room, which was not a good sign. Hide-and-seek was a favorite tactic of my daughter's whenever she knew she had done something wrong. Her trash bag sat in the middle of the bedroom. Full, from the look of it. I walked over and peered inside.

Tiny dresses and blankets were neatly folded and piled, along with a hanger or two she had missed. But no stuffed animals. I was ready to pronounce judgment and sentencing for disobeying me until I thought that perhaps the animals were in the bottom rather than on top; Sara had chosen to get the worst over with first. I shoved my arm down into the bag and rooted around. Sure enough, about midway through the bag cotton and polyester gave way to fur and felt.

I took out the clothes to see what she had chosen to give away. There was a Winnie the Pooh that had long ceased to capture her imagination, a stuffed pig she hadn't seen since it had been in her crib, and an assortment of giraffes and zebras. Not bad, I thought. Then the familiar sight of a brown arm caught my eye. I reached in again and dug to the bottom. What I pulled out shocked me.

Brown fur and eyes. Colored patches on the upper arms, legs, stomach, and backside. The tiny white T-shirt said "Juvenile Diabetes Research Foundation" across the front. A medical alert bracelet hung from its left wrist.

I held the toy in my hands. No, I decided, not *toy*—that was the wrong word.

This was Beary.

Sara had been diagnosed with type 1 diabetes just a few months prior, and my thoughts of her stay in the hospital still caused many sleepless nights. It was a horrible and confusing time, but at least Abby and I had the benefit of comprehension. We knew what had happened to our daughter. Sara had a disease. Her autoimmune system had attacked the beta cells in her pancreas, rendering it incapable of producing insulin. At five, though, Sara could not possibly know what was happening. She was unable to understand why she couldn't go home and why she had tubes going into her body and why she felt so sick. For five days she languished in her hospital bed, thirty miles from the safety and familiarity of home, in a constant state of fear.

Abby and I did our best to comfort her, but after two days

there was little we could do other than dry her tears and assure her everything would be okay, even if we still feared it wouldn't.

Then Beary showed up.

The nurse came into Sara's room on the third day of our stay. The hospital had a problem, she said. A bear had been found abandoned. Poor thing. No one had any idea where his mommy and daddy were. And to make things worse, the bear had diabetes. The doctors could tell because of the bracelet on his wrist and the patches on his body that showed where he could get his insulin shots.

It was a shame, the nurse said. A hospital was no place to raise a bear. But who could take him home? No one they knew. It certainly couldn't be an adult. What grown-up knows how to take care of a teddy bear? And besides, it was hard to find someone who could understand about having your sugar checked and getting shots every day.

"I can take him," Sara offered.

"What a wonderful idea!" said the nurse.

She brought the bear in and settled it into Sara's arms. Sara was like a mother receiving her firstborn. Beary, she named it. It was the first smile she'd shown in three days.

When she was finally discharged, Sara made sure Beary never left her side. When she ate, he ate. And when her sugar was checked she made sure his was checked, too. When she got her shots it was his arm she squeezed, and when it was his turn he squeezed hers. Beary needed her, Sara said. And that was true. But what she didn't say was also true—she needed him.

Which made the fact that Beary had been put into the trash bag so odd. It had to be a mistake, I thought. Had to.

It was a good thing I checked her bag before I left. I could see myself in the middle of the night rummaging through the small building at the firehouse where the clothes and stuffed animals were stored, trying in vain to find Beary and then having to tell Sara I couldn't.

"Sara?" I called.

She came bounding down the hallway and into her room. "Hi, Daddy," she said.

"Hey there. I was going through your bag and found this." I held the bear up in my hand. "Beary must've crawled in here by accident."

"No, he didn't," she said. "I put him in there."

"You did?"

"Yes."

"Honey, when I said you had to get rid of some of your stuffed animals, I just meant the ones you didn't play with anymore. You can't get rid of Beary."

"Why?" she asked.

"Because he's Beary. He's important to you."

"That's why I want to give him away."

"I don't understand, Sara. If he's important to you, then you should want to keep him. He helps you."

Sara stood in front of me, thinking. "Jesus loves poor people, right, Daddy?"

"That's right," I said.

"Does He love scared people, too?"

"Sure He does," I told her. "He loves them special."

"Did God make Beary for me so I wouldn't be scared in the hospital?"

The question caught me off guard. "Yes," I finally said.

"He helped me not be sad when I got diabetes, so he can help someone else not be sad when their house burns down."

We stared at one another, and I finally understood. "Okay," I said. "I'll put him back in there, then. If you're sure."

Sara said, "I'm sure. But I guess just take his shirt off. Maybe whoever gets him next won't have diabetes."

She ran off to the living room and her cartoons, leaving me alone with Beary.

In the end, Sara and I both succeeded in helping the poor and pained. In a lot of minds, that would be good enough. But as proud as I was by my actions, my intentions had fallen a little short. My bag had been filled with pants that were worn and faded and shirts that had long since gone out of style. They weren't good enough. Not for me. But they were good enough for the desperate.

But Sara knew the pain of need. Maybe not the needs of clothing or shelter, but certainly needs more basic—those of comfort and understanding. She had felt those needs during her five horrible days in the hospital, and she would likely feel them every day for the rest of her life. And it was that pain that had allowed her to give not out of duty, but love.

That was why Sara had chosen not to part with mere cast-offs and rejects, but with the one thing that represented the link between the innocence she longed to hold on to and the maturity her disease forced her to have.

I gently placed Beary back into the trash bag. He rested on a stuffed lion that pushed his paw up in a final wave.

Good-bye, he said. My work here is done. Don't worry, Sara knows what she's doing. She's a smart girl, you know.

You could learn a thing or two from her. Like how to give, for instance. And how to love. And how to make good out of the ugliness of your life.

And maybe most of all, how to realize that you are not a keeper of your blessings, but a borrower.

# 19

## The Plan

While Sara and Josh picked up the last of the toys straggling behind in the living room, Abby and I sat at the dining room table over coffee to decide what was next and what we could do about it.

I'd worried. I'd prayed. I'd thought. The answer eluded me. Abby seemed to think that putting in an application at the college wouldn't do any harm. If my job at the factory was saved by the *Exciting Announcement!!!* and I still wanted to stay, fine. If my job was lost, having a head start on other possibilities would be a prudent thing.

I agreed with her in principle. But prudence had never really been one of my strong points, and I couldn't ignore what was simmering beneath all of my feelings on the matter.

I'm always up for a good pity party. Since no one else ever worked up enough pity for me, it's one of those jobs I took upon myself. And I could always throw a great party. *Poor me. Poor, poor me.* It actually felt good. For a while.

The truth was that I felt like a nothing. A nothing who might lose his nothing job and so would go apply for another nothing job. *I should have been more by now.* More of *what* I didn't exactly know. Like most people, I knew more of what I was missing than what I wanted to find.

I was thankful for the blessings God had given me, blessings I was sure I didn't deserve. I knew I had a rich life, one more fulfilling than most could ask for. But was it a *good* life? A good life *for me*? Despite all I had, I couldn't answer yes to that question. And despite all I was, I knew what I lacked most in life. I wanted to stand out in some way. I wanted to be accomplished at something.

Men tend to define themselves by what they do for a living. Their jobs mark their places in the world. And while I didn't place that much emphasis on what I did for a living, I realized that every job I'd ever had never counted for much in the big picture. I needed meaning in what I did, and I'd had none of that. As I boy I had dreamed of being an astronaut, then a ballplayer. Those dreams were long dead now, victims of the reality of who I truly was—just a man. Not too bright and not too stupid, not too rich and not too poor, not too happy and not too sad. A middle-of-the-road, ordinary man. That was me. Nice to meet you.

And that should have all been good enough, I supposed. But it wasn't. There are two things every decent person possessed in his or her life, at least in my opinion. One is a set of lofty goals that rise just a bit higher than their reach. The other is a desire to do something good for this world. And it didn't look as though I was going to do that. I was too common.

My wife said in her kind and roundabout way that maybe I was thinking too much. That people leave their mark on the world through their family and friends. That all of what I'd said didn't change the fact that I should go and put in an application anyway. She said it would make me feel better about going back to work the next day. And if I hurried, I'd still have a little daylight left to take the kids outside again when I got back.

All good points.

So I put my boots back on. Abby suggested with a wink that I wear a different coat. Like any good husband ready to be done talking, I did so without asking why and headed for the door. I paused to tell her she was right but didn't tell her that maybe she was wrong. I didn't want to waste the life that God had given me, and I thought I was doing just that. The idea of getting a job in the lower echelons of a college only meant that I would be wasting it a little longer.


Twenty minutes plus the detour later, and the city loomed from my windshield. Stanley, Virginia, had a population of about twenty-four thousand people. As I made my way through the commercial areas toward downtown, every one of those twenty-four thousand was either driving the streets or walking the sidewalks.

The exaggeration was a product of the fact that I did not particularly like crowded areas and looked with suspicion upon those who did. And if by chance I ended up being offered the job, and if by chance I accepted said offer, I would by default have to spend much of the week smack in the middle of what I considered to be a pretty big city—something I intended to keep in mind as I navigated the crowd.

It had been a while since I had been downtown—a maze of one-way streets, steep hills, and hidden stop signs all designed to make fools out of everyone who wasn't familiar with the surroundings. After many wrong turns and a few right ones, I finally arrived at the front door.

Martha Barton College covered over fifty acres in the heart of the city and had done so since its founding in 1842. So said the historical preservation sign outside of the administrative building. Which, I soon found out, was not where I should go to fill out an application. For that, the nice receptionist said, I had to go to the physical plant building, which was about one mile and three hills away.

"Thank you," I told her.

"You're very welcome," she said. "Have a great day."

"You, too, ma'am."

"And happy holidays!"

I winced. Again with the happy holidays. I decided to let it slide this time. This was a college, I reasoned, and colleges are the bastions of political correctness. One must make concessions at times. Besides, I was still weary from my bout with the Christmas police at Super Mart earlier. And I didn't want to start throwing one of my fits in front of someone I might end up having to see every day.

"Merry Christmas," I said, smiling against saying anything more.

I decided to walk instead of drive, mostly because that way I didn't have to worry about the traffic flow. I popped a quarter into the parking meter and aimed myself at the nearest hill.

Either the receptionist's directions were a little fuzzy or my brain was, because I got lost soon thereafter. It didn't matter if my mind wandering led to my feet wandering or the other way around, but time had come to stop meandering and sharpen my sights on where both my feet and my life were headed.

That's what my whole snow day had come down to, after all—taking stock of my life.

As I walked among the quiet side streets of Stanley, vainly searching for something called a physical plant, I realized that was precisely what had happened to me. I had let my life get away from me. It seemed as though just a few months ago I was a senior in high school, sitting in class with Kenny McCallom, trying to write out what would become of my life. Had I made a life for myself? I didn't know.

For that essay in Mrs. Houser's class I had written out what I dubbed The Plan. It was the result of seventeen years of observation concerning what society thought was a successful life. It covered everything from finances (five hundred thousand dollars a year, minimum) to housing (a five-thousand-square-foot log home at the top of the mountain) to occupation (whatever made me rich) to vehicle (a Ferrari to drive into town, and an Aston Martin to drive back home).

I exhaled a sarcastic chuckle as I walked. Things hadn't really turned out the way I thought they would. Not that I ever really had a chance at any of those things anyway. But there was still the nagging thought that I had let someone down. Me? God? My family? I didn't know.

When I was a boy my father would drive us all out to Stanley and spend some time at the park, feeding the ducks and riding the train and such. We would always drive past the college on the way. I remembered thinking how wonderful the campus looked, how stately the buildings were. That was where the smart people were, I thought. The good people. And many times I dreamed of going there, either to study as a student or teach as a professor. And here I was, all these years later, about to fill out an application to become part of that ivory tower. Not as a student, though, or as a professor. But just to get a job to keep my family's heads above the water.

It was a sad thought, one that arrived the same time as a street sign. I suddenly knew where I was and where I was heading, both in body and in life.

South.

When the bumper stickers on the cars parked along the streets went from "God, Guns, and Guts Made America— Let's Keep All Three" and "Harley Rider for Life" to "Meat Is Murder" and "So Many Christians—So Few Lions," I knew I was close to the campus again.

The physical plant was located in an ancient building that overlooked an even more ancient soccer field. While most of the college seemed quiet, this little corner of campus was alive with activity. Pickups fitted with snowplows came and went. Workers armed with shovels and bags of salt paraded in and out the doors. I guessed these people didn't get snow days, either. Something else to keep in mind.

I walked through the door and up the stairs to the second floor, where I found a hallway lined with offices. I stood at the first one and was greeted by another nice receptionist whose nameplate said *Administrative Assistant*.

"I'd like an application, please," I said.

"Sure," she answered, pulling open a desk drawer and fishing one out. "You can have a seat out in the hallway. I'll take it when you're done. Do you need a pen?"

"No thanks, I have one."

"Okay, here you go," she said, handing me a ballpoint anyway.

"Thank you," I said, politely accepting it. I walked out into the bustling hallway and found a small table and chairs against the wall. I sat down and got as comfortable as I could.

Though I had started my working career at sixteen and had worked at five jobs over the next eighteen years, this was only the second time I had to fill out a job application. My first came when I applied to the factory. That application covered some five pages and was followed by a battery of tests that made me feel as though I was applying for fieldwork with the CIA rather than to perform the sort of mindless tasks that your average primate could master.

This application looked better. Two pages, front and back. A picture of the scales of justice was stamped at the top of the first page. "Attorney Developed" was written around it. The questions were pretty standard fare but by no means irrelevant. And I had to be honest in answering them, too. On the last page and above the blank for my signature was the "Applicant Statement." The last paragraph, written in red ink to signify its seriousness, said this: "I understand that any information provided by me that is found to be false, incomplete, or misrepresented in any respect will be sufficient cause to (i) eliminate me from further consideration for employment, or (ii) may result in my immediate discharge from the employer's service, whenever it is discovered."

So not only could I not lie, I couldn't half-lie or embellish, either.

I had just spent about twenty minutes wandering around

the streets of Stanley trying to figure out where I stood in life. What better way to measure my progress than to fill out a job application? An application, after all, deals in truth. And verifiable truth at that. There the hubris could be stripped away, leaving only the unmitigated facts of my life to be evaluated and judged on their own merits. Then I could see how my life matched up with The Plan.

This was serious business. I considered getting up and walking out rather than to face who I was and what I had become. Fear told me that filling out that application would prove me a failure once and for all. Better to just leave, go back home, and try again. Maybe tomorrow. Yes. There was always tomorrow.

But before I could ball up the application and stuff it into my pocket, Administrative Assistant popped her head out of the door.

"Hi there," she said.

"Hi."

"Just checking on you."

"I'm still here," I said, wishing I wasn't.

"Good," she said. "I'll take it when you're done. No rush."

"All right."

I wasn't stuck, but I didn't feel too good about leaving then, either. If I did, Administrative Assistant might be inclined to tell everyone the funny story about the idiot who tried to fill out an application, freaked out, and left. I'd always hated looking stupid in front of people. The only thing worse was looking stupid in front of people and not being around to defend myself.

So I took her pen and set to work, quickly checking yes or no to the easier questions, such as if I'd ever been convicted of a felony, if I was a legal citizen of the United States, and if I was looking for a part- or full-time position. So far, everything was going well. No surprises or disappointments. Maybe this wouldn't be so bad after all.

But I soon found that the questions left were ones I felt might pose a problem. If not to the college, then maybe to me.

"Name," for instance. I knew it was a ridiculous thing to stumble over but I did. I was applying for a job, after all, and it seemed as though the object was to stand out. My name did not stand out. It was boring. It was normal. I had always wanted a cool name, like Gunnar or Luke or Donovan. And Boyd? Please. There were so many Boyds in this valley and in the mountains around it that you couldn't throw a rock without hitting one of us. My name certainly hadn't gotten me very far in life. My name hadn't garnered me the recognition I longed for in high school. If it was pass or fail according to The Plan, then my name failed.

"Address" didn't bother me too much, but "How long have you lived at this location?" did. The brick ranch my family lived in was the first house my wife and I bought. Both of us had sworn our whole lives never to be stuck in a subdivision, so of course that's exactly where we ended up. Our house hadn't been built with things like functionality and family in mind. Instead, all of the rooms were cut off from one another and chopped up to the extent that even though we had almost two thousand square feet of living space, we could never have our families over for a get-together. Unless, of course, it was warm and we could go in our half-the-size-of-a-tennis-court backyard.

I wanted to move. I wanted to find a place farther out

in the country, where we could have a big yard and plant a garden. I didn't want a *house*. We had one of those. What I wanted was a *home*. Somewhere to stay for good. Somewhere our children could always come back to, no matter what. And we were finally all set to go and find one, too. But then all the mess with the factory started. Now it looked as though we'd better get comfortable where we were. *Log home at the top of the mountain*. Yeah. Right.

"Position applied for." Mailroom assistant—that's what was called for there. But I realized that if there was ever a job that seemed less glamorous and less meaningful than that of a factory worker, it was an assistant in the mailroom of a small college. I couldn't help but think that I was taking a few steps down rather than up life's ladder. I began to think of all the things I wished I could have written into that space. *Professor* was one. *Dean* of the college. *President*. I even made one up—*Executive Director for the Dispensing of Knowledge and Wisdom*. Except for the last one, of course, all of them were positions I maybe could have attained in life, if only I had done a few more things and left a few others undone. But it was not meant to be. Whether that was God's will or my own fault or a combination of the two wasn't clear. What was clear was that thus far working in a factory had been the pinnacle of my professional career, and even that looked to be nearly over. I scribbled "Mailroom assistant" into the blank. Another failure.

"What is your desired pay?" was next. A loaded question if there ever was one. My first job at the 7-Eleven in town had paid $4.15 an hour. Big bucks for a sixteen-year-old kid who lived at home. Not-so-big bucks for a sixteen-year-old kid who lived at home and had to put his own gas into his own vehicle. It didn't take too many paychecks for me to realize that I was barely making enough money to live on, which was a travesty given the amount of work I had to do. And thus I was taught my first of many great lessons in life—you're never going to get paid what you think you're worth.

As the years and jobs changed, though, so did my pay. Now at the factory I was making almost twenty-three dollars an hour. Pretty good money, as far as I was concerned. About as much as a guy like me could hope to make in that area. But that wasn't nearly as much as I'd hoped to make when I was in high school. If anything pointed more obviously to the fact that The Plan and my life were on two completely opposite tracks, it was my bank account.

I might have been an amateur at filling out job applications, but I was experienced enough to know that putting a number in that space spelled certain doom. I thought about putting "Enough to live on," but that sounded a little stupid. So I just wrote "Open" and left it at that. Still, in the grand scheme of things, it was another failure in my life.

"Employment History." I decided to limit this to the jobs I'd had since graduation from high school, which was a grand total of two. That could be seen as a good thing, I thought. Most people generally went through more than that after fifteen years out of high school, trying to find their niche. I always chalked it up to a sense of loyalty. Then again, it might just display a resistance to change that I'd had my entire life.

The factory came first.

Compensation (starting): $12/hour
Compensation (ending): $22.40/hour
Starting job title: Spinning operator

Final job title: Warper operator
Why did you leave? Still employed

What did you like most about your position? The money.
  [*It was serious business to be honest here.*]
What did you like least about this position? Everything
  else. [*Again, honesty.*]
Then there was my job before that, down at the Amoco in
  town.

Compensation (starting): $6/hour
Compensation (ending): $10/hour
Starting job title: Cashier
Final job title: Assistant manager

It looked good on paper, but in truth the title was more
ceremonial than anything else.

What did you like most about your position? Many of the
  people.
What did you like least about this position? A few of the
  people.

There. My fifteen years of post–high school work: a gas
station and a factory. I wasn't exactly doing something that
could get me fancy cars and a big house. Failure again.

"Skills and qualifications." Here I was supposed to list any
special training or skills that could assist me in performing
the position of Mailroom Assistant. That section truly did
stump me. Special training? I'd never had any special training in my life. Skills? Please. I didn't have any skills to set

myself apart from anyone else. If I was extraordinary at anything, it was my ordinariness. I left that section blank. Failure number six. I was on a roll.

"List special accomplishments, awards, etc." The last section. This was the one part of the application that could have
redeemed me in my own eyes. Here should have gone the
evidence that proved some part of The Plan was still alive.
It didn't have to be certain or likely, just *possible*. But again,
there was nothing to write down. I left that section blank as
well. Failure number seven.

My application was finished. All that was left was to add
my signature and turn it over to Administrative Assistant.
But I couldn't. Signing that application would make its contents official. It would say to whoever read it that I abided
by what I had written. This was me. This was my life. And I
didn't want it to be.

I wanted more. Not more things or more money. Not The
Plan. I had placed my life alongside it as a guide for measure-
ment, but I knew it wasn't The Plan that I wanted. Not anymore. That was simply the nonsensical definition of what an
inexperienced and gullible seventeen-year-old once thought
success in life meant. But still, I wanted more than I had. If
not The Plan, then surely a life that meant something and
counted for something. A life that mattered.

I wanted skills and qualifications. I had none. I wanted to
have accomplished something. I hadn't. I wanted an award for
a life well-lived. But I could receive no such award because I
didn't have a well-lived life. Not in my eyes. The only hope I
had, the only thing I held on to, was the fact that there was still
time for me. I had blown the first fifteen years after high school,
but that didn't mean I had to blow the next fifteen as well.

This, finally, was me. All me. And there just wasn't much I could do about it.

I pushed my pen across the paper to scribble my signature. It was done.

But it wasn't. The pen Administrative Assistant had given me had run out of ink. Wonderful. If that wasn't a sign, I didn't know what was. I reached into my pocket to pull out my own and pulled out a wad of something else.

Two pieces of paper and a toy car. How and when they got there I couldn't say. *What the...?* I thought. I carefully placed the items on the table and examined them.

First was the toy car. A Matchbox, not unlike the ones I played with when I was a child. But this was not your normal, everyday Matchbox car. This was Josh's favorite, Lightning McQueen. It was scratched and dented from constantly being thrown into one wall or another and worn from repeated use, evidence that the car was my son's life and constant companion. He slept with it at night and fed it imaginary oil and gas at the table and washed it along with himself in the bathtub. He never went anywhere without it. And yet here it was. With me.

The next item was a small piece of folded construction paper from Sara. On the front were two stick figures. One wore a hat and was tall. "Dady" was written over it. The other was shorter and had blond hair. "Sara" was written over that one. We were holding hands and smiling. On the inside and in another hand was written "Best daddy in the world." Under it, for authenticity, was Sara's name again. Also flowers, the sun, and a rainbow.

The last item was a small, folded piece of paper from my wife. "Good luck," the note said. "Remember that we love you."

Then it hit me. They must have put those things in my coat pocket sometime during my trip to Super Mart. That was why my wife wanted me to switch coats before I left for the college. She knew I would need the contents of that pocket.

"Remember that we love you."

With reminders like that, how could I forget?

Leave it to my family to pick me up out of the doldrums. Leave it to them to put a smile on my face even though they didn't know I needed one. If someone had walked by just then, they would have just seen a pile of scribbles and a junk toy. Food for the trash can. But to me they were much, much more.

Though I couldn't use them on my application, there in front of me sat proof that my life wasn't such a failure after all. They wanted accomplishments? How about earning my child's faith so much that he trusted me with his most valuable possession? They wanted awards? I was "Best daddy in the world" and had won the hand of my wife. How much better did it get than that?

It was then I realized that though the application I had just filled out could display the facts of my life, it could not display the truths of it. I had plenty of evidence to corroborate the theory that I had turned out to be a disappointment. But this was one of those times when all of the evidence, however compelling, still led to the wrong conclusion.

For instance: true, my name was not a unique one on the surface. There were, after all, about a half dozen Peter Boyds in the valley. But *this* Peter Boyd was named after his father, the greatest man I ever knew, and an uncle who had died long before I was born. My father was close to his uncle, and his death was devastating. To be named after a well-loved relative you've never met might not mean much to some people. To me, it was an honor.

And though my wife and I had lived in the same old house for eleven years in a neighborhood we swore we would never move into, that house still held many wonderful memories. It was the house our children first came home to from the hospital when they were born. Sara's tiny hand- and foot-prints were still painted along the walls of her bedroom. And in Josh's room, a Winnie the Pooh mural was painted by myself, my wife, and a close neighbor who had since moved. Our house kept us warm and cool and dry. There had been much laughter there, and much sadness. To move away to a log home in the mountains would be wonderful, yes. But it would be awfully hard, too.

And on second thought, I didn't think I was professor material, or dean. Certainly not president. And if there were ever a position I was underqualified to hold, Executive Director for the Dispensing of Wisdom and Knowledge was it. I was always more the kind of person who stuck in the background. I was a watcher more than a doer. I was a stagehand in life. I kept things running along so the actors could flaunt themselves and the show could go on. Sort of like a mailroom assistant.

Desired pay? How much did I really need as long as I had a place to stay, food to eat, clothes to wear, and people to love?

And yes, all I'd managed to get since high school was one job at a gas station and another at a factory. So what? Because of those things I'd gained friendships that would last my entire life. Because of them I'd gathered enough stories to last through my grandchildren. Sure, not all of the memories from those places were good ones. But where can you find only good memories?

"Skills and qualifications"? Maybe none that stood out. But give me the time and I could make most people laugh at least once. And I was usually, eventually able to see the brighter side of things. And I was trustworthy. All useful things, whether in a job or in a life.

Maybe I wasn't an example of success in the eyes of the world. But maybe that didn't matter. Maybe what mattered was being a success in the eyes of God and the ones you loved the most in this life.

I reached into my pocket again for my pen and found it that time. I then signed my name across the bottom of the application. It was a big, bold signature. I wanted the person who read it to see my name. I wanted them to see that I was proud of the life I'd had. Proud of the blessings God had seen fit to give me.

In the end, it didn't matter that I might lose my job. That was out of my hands. And it didn't matter that things had to look so bleak at Christmastime. Maybe Santa's sack would be a little lighter this year. So what? Come Christmas morning, what was under the tree didn't matter nearly as much as who was gathered around it.

I got up and took the application back to Administrative Assistant.

"All done?" she asked.

"Yes, ma'am," I answered.

"Great. We'll get back to you."

"Fine. Have a good day."

"You, too," she said. "And Merry Christmas."

*Merry Christmas*, she said. God bless her.

"It sure is," I said.

# 20

*The Detour*

The sun had begun its long good-bye to the day as I made my way home. In another couple of hours it would set behind the mountains, casting streaks of orange and purple against the still-lingering clouds, and be gone. Gone, too, would be my snow day. It was a shame; seldom did life grant what amounted to a time-out to catch your breath and remember some things you had maybe forgotten. But of course all things must end at some point, if only so they could be made new again later on. I managed to convince myself that was the case with that day. It would be made new again. There would be other snow days, I promised myself. Ones even better than the one I'd just had.

In the meantime, I would have to tend to the business at hand. I knew I could well stroll into work the next day and be told that while my contribution to the company was appreciated, my services were no longer needed. There would, no doubt, be some rough times ahead, times that would likely test whatever hope and faith I had left. But those times would also end at some point. Night lasts for only so long. The sun will rise again. Such was our existence upon this earth, alternating seasons of trial and joy that ultimately either wore us down or built us up. As with much of life, the choice was ours.

The kids would be wondering where I was. Dinner was probably being fixed. I wanted to go home. As enjoyable as my day had been, I was exhausted. But between the stoplight where I was sitting and home was the detour. Again.

As I sat there waiting for the light to go from red to green and thinking about the next day at work, I realized that my life had just taken a detour as well. Like the road that led home, the road through life I thought I should be traveling on was blocked. Maybe there was construction going on in my life, too. Maybe God was doing some improvements to make my ride a little smoother later on. I didn't know. The department of transportation was saying I had to take the long way around to get where I wanted to be. God seemed to be saying the same thing. I wasn't very fond of either of them right then.

But just when my mood was about to turn really ugly, I drove past a little mom-and-pop store. The owners sold Amish-made furniture mostly, along with an assortment of quilts, pictures, and homemade toys. In the warmer months they would sometimes offer horse rides and sell some pretty good barbeque chicken, too. A marquee out by the road was usually reserved for the newest sale items or the hours of operation. But all of that had been taken down in favor of a small bit of wisdom, no doubt placed there to soothe the rage of all the other people besides me who were being forced to take the long way around.

*The Best Things in Life May Be Discovered on a Detour*, it said.

Those words hit me with enough force to almost take my breath. And more than that, those words were true. I never would have experienced my snow day if it weren't for the detour at work. If everything had been fine there, if the company had been purring along nicely and my job had been firmly in place, I would have likely gone to work that morning instead of staying home. I would have missed seeing Santa at the Super Mart, playing with the kids in the snow, and witnessing Mikey's trip down the hill. I would have never met Eleanor, seen Kenny, or maybe repaired some bridges with Bobby Barnes. I would have never driven over to Stanley to fill out a job application and realized that I was really better off than I ever thought I'd be. I would have missed out on those things and all the other things I'd seen and done that taught me success wasn't measured by the things I could afford to get, but by the things I could afford to give.

There were things like love, for instance. And time. And dreams and hope and company. We were all rich in those, wealthy beyond measure, but each day we chose to cast all the wealth aside and live in the poverty of worldly gain. What crazy people we were. No wonder the world was so messed up. We had everything backwards. We were all living outside in with the hope that what we surrounded ourselves with would make us better people. We needed to live inside out with the hope that what came out of us would make the world better.

I drove past Mandy's house on the way up to my street.

She and Jack were out in the yard, throwing snowballs at each other and laughing. I remembered the bread and milk that had started my day. That was what it all came down to—the necessities of life. As long as we had those, nothing else really mattered and everything else could be borne.

I pulled up to our mailbox by the driveway. Inside were the usual bills and junk mail, along with a few Christmas cards. I paused to survey the scene in front of me. A Christmas tree glittered through the living room window. Bows and greenery adorned the porch. And there, everywhere, were three pairs of footprints. Two small and one not so small, winding their way through the yard and ending at the front porch. Remnants of my exposition with the children. That walk may have just been the best part of my day, though to look at the evidence left behind one would think that we had simply wandered around without purpose. Not true. There was a reason to our walk. We weren't out to find anything, really, but to just enjoy the looking.

And the children had no worries about where we were all going. They had their father with them, after all. Their father saw what was ahead. He saw where they could go, where the slick parts were, and where the ice was falling off the trees. He knew what to steer them around and what was okay for them to go through. All they had to do was go one step at a time.

My eyes followed the footprints. Like them, my life seemed to twist and turn, sometimes gradually and sometimes suddenly. I supposed that I was on a journey as well. And though the evidence sometimes looked as though I was simply wandering around without purpose, I knew that wasn't the case. I worried about where I was headed and what was going to happen, but I didn't have to. I had my Father with me, after all. He saw what was ahead. He knew where the dangerous parts were. He knew what to steer me around and what was okay for me to go through. All I had to do was go one step at a time.

Sometimes it wasn't all about the finding, but the looking.

The front door was flung open then. Two small children ran out onto the porch and began waving. At the window was their mother, my wife, smiling.

Pay attention. Laugh. Wonder. That was what our walk around the yard was all about. It was what my walk around this life was all about, too. And if I followed the tracks of both, I would see they eventually led to the same place.

Home.

# Epilogue

The great thing about a small town is that you get to be a constant observer of so many unfolding stories. There is no crime, no traffic jams or scandals. No distractions. Nothing to do but visit and talk and ponder. You get to know people. You get to share their lives in big ways and little. You watch them live their tale as you live your own.

Mandy and Jack moved last year. They now rent a house on a dairy farm outside of town. Jack seems to have a mind for cows and fields and such and is planning on doing a little farming of his own one day. The two of them are doing fine. We miss them in the neighborhood, but it's a little quieter out on the farm, she says. And, of course, there is always plenty of milk around.

I still go to Super Mart, and often. The prices there are still good and the people there are still peculiar, which makes it a perfect place to spend some time. I have yet to run into

Helen and Charlie again, but I did get a "Merry Christmas" from the cashier there a few weeks ago. It wasn't from Carrie. She has since moved on, I suppose.

I never saw the Super Mart Santa again, either, though I still scan the parking lot for him every time I stop there. Last year I decided to take up his mantle and deliver a little of my own Christmas magic. The results were…unexpected. But that is another story for another time. Still, if you ever happen to find a gift in your vehicle with a small note attached, don't look up toward the sky for a sleigh, look out toward the road for a truck.

Speaking of which, I still dress up as Santa for the kids every Christmas. It is, hands down, the highlight of every Christmas. My children can hear all the talk their friends dish out. They *know* there is a Santa. And they have irrefutable proof, too. Their mother has luckily had a video camera in her hand and happened to tape the children every Christmas Eve when Santa peeked through the window. Sooner or later they will realize that I never happen to be around when Saint Nick makes his yearly appearance. I'm still trying to figure out how I can get around this.

Kenny McCallom quit his job stocking shelves at Super Mart and took a job selling cars. He's doing pretty well at it, too. From what I understand the family has moved into their first home. Turns out he found his comfort without the aid of a college education, which he decided to put on hold. I heard his oldest daughter was diagnosed with type 1 diabetes a few months ago. I also heard she was a pretty sharp girl. Maybe she'll be the one to find a cure. Let's all hope and pray.

Bobby Barnes is still playing hide-and-seek with God, though I think it's getting a little harder for him to hide. He sold his business a few months after I passed him on the road, and word has it that he filed for bankruptcy. I haven't seen him around lately. But if I do, I'll say hey. You never know.

Eugene Turner is still fixing gutters and unclogging sinks and loving every minute of it.

Sara and Josh still play with the Lite Brite. Between you and me, I still play with it, too. Because sometimes I still need to be reminded that the holes in our lives are there so the light can shine through. The mysterious holes in our yard by the oak tree reappeared the next year. Against the children's wishes, I filled them in with gravel and sand again and then put big rocks on top of them. That's seemed to put an end to the mystery. The rocks are still there and the holes are still not. I know, I know, I said mystery is good. And it is. I just didn't like the idea of a critter I didn't know making its home in our yard.

I buried an arrowhead in the sandbox a few days later. Another mystery. Whose was it? Where did it come from? *Pocahontas*, thought Sara. *Geronimo*, thought Josh. Were there more? Absolutely, they found out, once another one mysteriously appeared near the swing set a few days after that. My wife and I now have two little Indiana Joneses running around the yard digging for treasure. Wonderful, I say.

Mikey Pannill and the other kids gave up sledding once the church put a new building on the hill. That's okay, though. Mikey now rides motorcycles. How in the world he managed to talk his mother into that I do not know, but I do know that he always wears a helmet and pads. Not a mouthpiece, though. Riding motorcycles is fun, and he couldn't laugh while wearing a mouthpiece.

Eleanor passed on a few months after our first talk. That

would be a sad thing to share if it weren't for what happened just before she died. It seems as though the company she lacked in this life was all made up for in the next. According to the nurses who tended to her final moments, Eleanor's last words were, "There are angels everywhere."

Chris Davies is getting a crash course in both the rules of the road and the rules of life. Back in the spring he drove past a speed trap going seventy in a thirty-five. Instead of yielding to the flashing blue lights and pulling over, Chris decided he could outrun his pursuer. It was a few minutes and about five miles later, after his Mustang had been wrapped around a tree and the state police were standing over him, that he finally realized he wasn't Bo Duke. "I didn't get scared," he told me later, "until I saw the gun in my face." And on top of all that, Heather the cheerleader broke up with him. She said she had to find herself. That'll take a while, I think.

After three days of languishing in the hallway closet—just to make sure—Beary was delivered to the firehouse. His whereabouts are currently unknown, and I'll admit I've spent some time wondering where he is. If you happen to know, drop us a line.

As for me, I went back to work the next day and found that my job was still there. All that worrying for nothing. Then a week later, two things happened. One was that I was told I would be cut out of my area and sent to another part of the factory and to a worse work schedule. The other was that I received a phone call from the college. I went to an interview and must have answered all the questions pretty well, because they offered me the job two weeks later. I said goodbye to the factory and hello to the college.

It hasn't been bad. Oh yes, the Boyds are now pinching

pennies and squeezing dimes, but God has a way of working things out just fine if you let Him. That's the key, I've found—letting Him. Of course, I still zig and zag and question where I'm going every once in a while, but I'm trying to do better and I suppose that's what matters. I'm home with my family every evening and there are no more weekends to work. I had eleven days off for Christmas this year. And though I have to work in the city, I have a real nice view of the mountains outside my windows. The people who have the crazy ideas, I've also found, are far outnumbered by the people who have the right ideas. There are many good people here, and more than a few wonderful ones.

I've found something else here that I seemed to lack at the factory—a sense of perspective. You could say that my presence here serves an important function. Turns out, handling all the mail for a college is a pretty big responsibility. A lot of people depend on me to do my job and do it well. I like that.

But according to the handbook sitting in the drawer of my office desk, I'm still classified as "nonessential personnel." I like that, too. I like knowing that while I'm necessary, I'm not essential. It's not all about me. There's comfort in that. So much of my life has always been about looking inward. About seeing things as they affected *me* rather than everyone else. I know better now. I know that life should be lived outside in as much as inside out. That we should affect the world as much as it affects us.

Being nonessential has another benefit, too. It offers me something I haven't had much of for the last twenty years. Something I plan on taking full advantage of as often as God and the weather see fit.

Snow days.

31901047510088